Bebés

Prayers for the Stolen

BY THE SAME AUTHOR

FICTION

A True Story Based on Lies

A Salamander-Child

The Poison that Fascinates

NON-FICTION

Widow Basquiat

POETRY

The Next Stranger

Newton's Sailor

Lady of the Broom

New & Selected Poems

Prayers for the Stolen

JENNIFER CLEMENT

HOGARTH
LONDON · NEW YORK

Published by Hogarth 2014

2 4 6 8 10 9 7 5 3 1

First published in Great Britain in 2014 by Hogarth
Random House, 20 Vauxhall Bridge Road,
London SW1V 2SA
www.randomhouse.co.uk

Addresses for companies within The Random House Group Limited can be found at: www.randomhouse.co.uk/offices.htm

The Random House Group Limited Reg. No. 954009

A CIP catalogue record for this book is available from the British Library

ISBN 9781781090176

The Random House Group Limited supports the Forest Stewardship Council® (FSC®), the leading international forest certification organisation. Our books carrying the FSC label are printed on FSC®-certified paper. FSC is the only forest certification scheme endorsed by the leading environmental organisations, including Greenpeace. Our paper procurement policy can be found at www.randomhouse.co.uk/environment

Typeset in Nexus Serif by Palimpsest Book Production Limited,
Falkirk, Stirlingshire

Printed and bound in Great Britain by
Clays Ltd, St Ives plc

For Richard and Sylvia

Part One

One

Now we make you ugly, my mother said. She whistled. Her mouth was so close she sprayed my neck with her whistle-spit. I could smell beer. In the mirror I watched her move the piece of charcoal across my face. It's a nasty life, she whispered.

It's my first memory. She held an old cracked mirror to my face. I must have been about five years old. The crack made my face look as if it had been broken into two pieces. The best thing you can be in Mexico is an ugly girl.

My name is Ladydi Garcia Martínez and I have brown skin, brown eyes, and brown frizzy hair, and look like everyone else I know. As a child my mother used to dress me up as a boy and call me Boy.

I told everyone a boy was born, she said.

If I were a girl then I would be stolen. All the drug traffickers had to do was hear that there was a pretty girl around and they'd sweep onto our lands in black Escalades and carry the girl off.

On television I watched girls getting pretty, combing their hair and braiding it with pink bows or wearing makeup, but this never happened in my house.

Maybe I need to knock out your teeth, my mother said.

As I grew older I rubbed a yellow or black marker over the white enamel so that my teeth looked rotten.

There is nothing more disgusting than a dirty mouth, Mother said.

It was Paula's mother who had the idea of digging the holes. She lived across from us and had her own small house and field of papaya trees.

My mother said that the state of Guerrero was turning into a rabbit warren with young girls hiding all over the place.

As soon as someone heard the sound of an SUV approaching, or saw a black dot in the distance or two or three black dots, all girls ran to the holes.

This was in the state of Guerrero. A hot land of rubber plants, snakes, iguanas and scorpions, the blond, transparent scorpions, which were hard to see and that kill. Guerrero had more spiders than any place in the world we were sure, and ants. Red ants that made our arms swell up and look like a leg.

This is where we are proud to be the angriest and meanest people in the world, Mother said.

When I was born, my mother announced to her neighbors and people in the market that a boy had been born.

Thank God a boy was born! she said.

Yes, thank God and the Virgin Mary, everyone answered even though no one was fooled. On our mountain only boys were born, and some of them turned into girls around the age of eleven. Then these boys had to turn into ugly girls who sometimes had to hide in holes in the ground.

We were like rabbits that hid when there was a hungry stray dog in the field, a dog that cannot close his mouth, and its tongue already tastes their fur. A rabbit stomps its back leg and this danger warning travels through the ground and alerts the other rabbits in the warren. In our area a warning was impossible since we all lived scattered and too far apart from each other. We were always on the lookout, though, and tried to learn to hear things that were very far away. My mother would bend her head down, close her eyes and concentrate on listening for an engine or the disturbed sounds that birds and small animals made when a car approached.

No one had ever come back. Every girl who had been stolen never returned or even sent a letter, my mother said, not even a letter. Every girl, except for Paula. She came back one year after she'd been taken.

From her mother, over and over again, we heard how she had been stolen. Then one day Paula walked back home. She had seven earrings that climbed up the cupped edge of her left ear in a straight line of blue, yellow and green studs and a tattoo that snaked around her wrist with the words *Cannibal's Baby*.

Paula just walked down the highway and up the dirt path to her house. She walked slowly, looking down, as if she were following a row of stones straight to her home.

No, my mother said. She was not following stones, that girl just smelled her way home to her mother.

Paula went into her room and lay down in her bed that was still covered with a few stuffed animals. Paula never spoke a word about what had happened to her. What we knew was that Paula's mother fed her from a bottle, gave her a milk bottle, actually sat her on her lap and gave her a baby bottle. Paula was fifteen then because I was fourteen. Her mother also bought her Gerber baby foods and fed her straight into her mouth with a small white plastic spoon from a coffee she bought at the OXXO shop at the gas station that was across the highway.

Did you see that? Did you see Paula's tattoo? my mother said.

Yes. Why?

You know what that means, right? She belongs. Jesus, Mary's son and Son of God, and the angels in heaven protect us all.

No, I didn't know what that meant. My mother did not want to say, but I found out later. I wondered how did someone get stolen from a small hut on a mountain by a drug trafficker, with a shaved head and a machine gun in one hand and a gray grenade in his back pocket, and end up being sold like a package of ground beef?

I watched out for Paula. I wanted to talk to her. She never left her house now but we had always been best friends, along with Maria and Estefani. I wanted to make her laugh and remember how we used to go to church on Sundays dressed up like boys and that my name had been Boy and her name had been Paulo. I wanted to remind her of the times we used to look at the soap-opera magazines together because she loved to look at the pretty clothes the television stars wore. I also wanted to know what had happened.

What everyone did know was that she had always been the prettiest girl in these parts of Guerrero. People said Paula was even prettier than the girls from Acapulco, which was a big compliment, as anything that was glamorous or special had to come from Acapulco. So the word was out.

Paula's mother dressed her in dresses stuffed with rags to make her look fat but everyone knew that less than one hour from the port of Acapulco, there was a girl living on a small property with her mother and three chickens who was more beautiful than Jennifer Lopez. It was just a matter of time. Even though Paula's mother thought up the idea of hiding girls in holes in the ground, which we all did, she was not able to save her own daughter.

One year before Paula was stolen, there had been a warning.

It was early in the morning when it happened. Paula's mother, Concha, was feeding old tortillas to her three chickens when she heard the sound of an engine down the road. Paula was still in bed fast asleep. She was in bed with her face washed clean, her hair roped into a long black braid that, during the night sleep, had coiled around her neck.

Paula was wearing an old T-shirt. It hung down below her knees, was made of white cotton and said the words *Wonder Bread* across the front in dark blue letters. She was also wearing a pair of pink panties, which my mother always said was worse than being naked!

Paula was deeply asleep when the narco barged into the house.

Concha said she'd been feeding the chickens, those three good-for-nothing chickens that had never laid an egg in all their lives, when she saw the tan-colored BMW coming up the narrow dirt path. For a second she thought it was a bull or some animal that had run away from the Acapulco zoo because she had not expected to see a light brown vehicle coming toward her.

When she'd thought of narcos coming, she always imagined the black SUVs with tinted windows, which were supposed to be illegal but everyone had them fixed so the cops could not look inside. Those black Cadillac Escalades with four doors and black windows filled with narcos and machine guns were like the Trojan Horse, or so my mother used to say.

How did my mother know about Troy? How did a

Mexican woman living all alone with one daughter in the Guerrero countryside, less than an hour from Acapulco by car and four hours by mule, know anything about Troy? It was simple. The one and only thing my father ever bought her when he came back from the United States was a small satellite dish antenna. My mother was addicted to historical documentaries and to Oprah's talk shows. In my house there was an altar to Oprah beside the one she had for the Virgin of Guadalupe. My mother did not call her Oprah. That is a name she never figured out. My mother called her Opera. So it was Opera this and Opera that.

In addition to documentaries and Oprah, we must have watched *The Sound of Music* at least a hundred times. My mother was always on the lookout to see when the movie would be programmed on a movie channel.

Every time Concha would tell us what had happened to Paula, the story was different. So we never knew the truth.

The drug trafficker who went to the house before Paula was stolen only went to get a good look at her. He went to see if the rumors were true. They were true.

It was different when Paula was stolen.

On our mountain, there were no men. It was like living where there were no trees.

It is like being a person with one arm, my mother said. No, no, no, she corrected herself. Being in a place without men is like being asleep without dreams.

Our men crossed the river to the United States. They dipped their feet in the water and waded up to their waists but they were dead when they got to the other side. In that river they shed their women and their children and walked into the great big USA cemetery. She was right. They sent money; they came back once or twice and then that was that. So on our land we were clumps of women working and trying to raise ourselves up. The only men around inhabited SUVs, rode motorcycles and appeared from out of nowhere with an AK-47 hanging from their shoulder, a bag of cocaine in the back pocket of their jeans and a pack of Marlboro Reds in their front shirt pocket. They wore Ray-Ban sunglasses and we had to make sure we never looked into their eyes, never saw the small black pupils that lay there and was the path inside their minds.

On the news we once heard about the kidnapping of thirty-five farmers who were picking corn in fields when some men with three large trucks drove up and stole all of them. The kidnappers pointed guns at the farmers and told them to get into the trucks. The farmers were in the trucks standing pressed together like cattle. The farmers returned to their homes after two or three weeks. They had been warned that if they talked about what had happened, they would be killed. Everyone knew they were stolen to be field hands and pick a marijuana crop.

If you were quiet about something then it never happened. Someone would write a song about it for sure. Everything you're not supposed to know about, or talk about, eventually turned up in a song.

Some idiot is going to write a song about those kidnapped farmers and get himself killed, my mother said.

On weekends my mother and I went to Acapulco where she worked as a cleaning lady for a rich family who lived in Mexico City. The family went to the holiday resort a couple of weekends a month. For years this family used to drive, but then they bought a helicopter. It took several months to build the helipad on their property. First they had to fill in the swimming pool with dirt and cover it up and then move the new swimming pool over a few feet.

They also relocated the tennis courts so that the heliport would be as far as possible from the house.

My father had also worked in Acapulco. He was a waiter at a hotel before he left for the States. He came back to Mexico a few times to visit us but then he never came back. My mother knew that it was the last time when the last time came.

This is the last time, she said.

What do you mean, Mama?

Look at him hard in the face; drink him up, because you're never going to see your daddy again. Guaranteed. Guaranteed.

She liked to use that word.

When I asked her how she knew he was not coming back she said, You just wait, Ladydi, you just wait and you'll see I'm right.

But how do you know? I asked again.

Let's see if you can figure it out, she answered.

It was a test. My mother liked to give tests and finding out why my father was not coming back was a test.

I began to observe him. I watched the way he did things around our small house and garden. I followed him as if he were a stranger that could steal something from me if I looked away.

One night I knew my mother had been right. It was so hot even the moon was warming our piece of the planet. I went outside and joined my father as he smoked a cigarette.

God, this place must be one of the hottest places on earth, he said as he exhaled the tobacco smoke from his mouth and nostrils at the same time.

He placed his arm around me and his skin was even hotter than mine. We could sear into each other.

And then he said it.

You and your mama are too good for me. I don't deserve you.

I passed the test with an A.

Son of a bitch, my mother said again and again, for years. She never said his name again. He was Son of a Bitch forever after.

Like many people on our mountain, my mother believed in hexes.

May a wind blow out the candle of his heart. May a gigantic termite grow in his navel, or an ant in his ear, she said. May his penis be eaten by a worm.

Then my father stopped sending us a monthly stipend from the USA. I guess we were also too good for his money.

Of course the USA to Mexico rumor road was the most powerful rumor route in the whole world. If you did not know the truth, you knew the rumor and the rumor was always a lot, lot more than the truth.

I'll take a rumor over the truth, my mother said.

The rumor that came from a Mexican restaurant in New York to a slaughterhouse in Nebraska, to a Wendy's restaurant in Ohio, to an orange field in Florida, to a hotel in San Diego, then crossed the river, in an act of resurrection, to a bar in Tijuana, to a marijuana field outside Morelia, to a glass-bottom boat in Acapulco, to a canteen in Chilpancingo and up our dirt road to the shade of our orange tree was that my father had another family 'over there'.

'Over here' was our story, but it was also everyone's story.

Over here we lived alone in our shack surrounded by all the objects my mother had stolen for years. We had dozens of pens and pencils, salt shakers and eyeglasses, and we had one large plastic garbage bag filled with little sugar packets she had stolen from restaurants. My mother never left a bathroom without taking the roll of toilet paper hidden in her bag. She didn't call it stealing, but my father did. When he was still with us and they used to fight, he said he lived with a thief. My mother believed that she was a borrower but I knew she never gave anything back. Her friends knew they had to hide everything. No matter where we would go, when we returned to our home the stuff was going to appear from out of her pockets, between her breasts and even from her hair. She had a knack for pushing stuff into it. I'd seen her pull small coffee spoons and spools of thread from her frizzy mane. Once she had a Snickers chocolate bar she'd stolen from Estefani's house. She'd pushed the candy bar up under her ponytail. She even stole from her very own daughter. I gave up thinking that anything belonged to me.

When my father left, my mother, who had never placed a lock on her mouth, said, That Son of a Bitch! Here we lose our men, we get AIDS from them, from their US whores, our daughters are stolen, our sons leave, but I love this country more than my own breath.

Then she said the word Mexico very slowly, and again, Mexico. It was as if she licked up the word off a plate.

Ever since I was a child my mother had told me to say a prayer for some thing. We always did. I had prayed for the clouds and pajamas. I had prayed for light bulbs and bees.

Don't ever pray for love and health, Mother said. Or money. If God hears what you really want, He will not give it to you. Guaranteed.

When my father left my mother said, Get down on your knees and pray for spoons.

Two

I only went to school until the end of primary. I was a boy most of that time. Our school was a little room down the hill. Some years teachers never showed up because they were scared to come to this part of the country. My mother said that any teacher who wanted to come here must be a drug trafficker or an idiot.

Nobody trusted anyone.

My mother said that every person was a drug dealer including the police, of course, the mayor, guaranteed, and even the damn president of the country was a narco.

My mother did not need to be asked questions, she asked them herself.

How do I know the president is a drug trafficker? she asked. He lets all the guns come in from the United States. Why doesn't he put the army on the border and stop the guns, huh? And, anyway, what is a worse thing to hold in your hand: a plant, a marijuana plant, a poppy, or a gun? God made the plants but man made the guns.

My school friends were the friends I've always had. There were only nine of us in first grade. My closest friends were Paula, Estefani, and Maria. We went to school with our hair cut short and in boys' clothes. All of us except for Maria.

Maria was born with a harelip and so her parents were not worried that she would be stolen.

When my mother talked about Maria she said, The harelip rabbit on the moon came down from the moon to our mountain.

Maria was also the only one of us who had a brother. His name was Miguel, but we called him Mike. He was four years older than Maria and everyone spoiled him because he was the only boy on our mountain.

Paula, as we all said, looked like Jennifer Lopez, but more beautiful.

Estefani had the blackest skin ever. In the state of Guerrero we are all very dark but she was like a piece of the night or a rare black iguana. Estefani was also tall and skinny and, since no one in Guerrero was tall, she stood out like the tallest tree in a wood. She saw things I never could see; even far-off things like cars coming down the highway. Once she saw a little black-red-and-white-striped snake curled up in a tree. It turned out that was a coral snake. These are snakes that want to drink the breast milk of sleeping mothers.

When you grow up in Guerrero you learn that anything that is red is dangerous and so we knew that snake was bad. Estefani said the snake had looked at her straight in the eye. She only told this to Paula, Maria, and me, just the three of us (her three best friends) because she knew it meant she was cursed. And she was, of course, as cursed as if the snake had been the evil fairy godmother with a wand who said your dreams will never come true.

When Maria was born with the harelip everyone was shocked. Her mother, Luz, kept her daughter inside the house and her father walked out the front door and never came back.

My mother liked to tell everyone what they should do. She did not mind her own business. So, she walked over to Maria's house to take a good look at the baby. I only know this story because my mother told it to me many times over. She looked at little Maria lying in Luz's arms covered by a white veil of gauze. She lifted the cloth and looked down at the baby.

She was born inside-out, like an inside-out sweater. You just need to get her turned back around, Mother said. I'll go and register her at the clinic.

My mother turned and walked down the mountain and took a bus to the clinic in Chilpancingo and registered the birth of Maria. This was done so that the local clinics would know which children in the rural area needed these kinds of operations. Doctors came from Mexico City every few years to operate for free but the patients had to be registered at birth.

It took eight years before a group of doctors came to Chilpancingo. A convoy of soldiers escorted them so that they would be protected from the drug traffickers' violent confrontations. Of course, by this time, we were all used to Maria's face. Because of this, some of her friends did not want her to have the operation. We wanted her to be happy and normal but her inside-out face made us fear the gods, made us aware of terrible punishments, made us think that something had gone wrong in our magic circle of people. She had become mythical like a drought or a flood. Maria was used as an example of God's wrath. Could a doctor fix that wrath? we wondered. Maria inhabited her myth and even began to look as if she was made of stone.

We thought Maria was powerful. My mother never thought it was power.

She's looking for an accident and she's going to find one, Mother said.

Estefani, Paula and I felt that the worst had already happened to Maria and so she was not afraid of anything, like the snake Estefani saw in the tree. It was Maria who picked up a long stick and poked at it until the snake fell to the ground. Estefani, Paula, and I shrieked and moved away, but Maria leaned over, picked it up, and held it between her thumb and index finger.

She looked at the snake and said, So you think you have an ugly face, well, look at my face!

Stop it, stop it, Paula said. It's going to bite you!

Idiot, that's what I want, Maria said and dropped the snake on the ground.

She called everyone an idiot. It was her favorite word.

One day when I was seven years old, Maria and I were walking home together from school. Usually we all left school together and would meet our mothers down on the highway and then branch out toward our different houses. This time, I can't remember why, Maria and I were alone. The school year was almost over and we were sad because the teacher who had come from Mexico City for a year was leaving and a new volunteer would be coming in September. In the countryside the people depended on volunteers from the city. We had volunteer teachers, social workers, doctors and nurses. They came as part of their required social work training. After a while we learned not to get too attached to these people who, as my mother said, come and go like salespeople with nothing to sell except the words *you must.*

I don't like people who come from far away, she said.

They have no idea of who we are, telling us you must do this and you must do that and you must do this and you must do that. Do I go to the city and tell them the place stinks and ask them, Hey, where's the grass and since when is the sky yellow? It's all just like the damn Roman Empire.

I didn't know what she meant by this, but I did know she'd been watching a documentary on the history of Rome.

I had that walk alone with Maria in the month of July. I remember the heat and the sadness of losing our teacher. It was very humid and my body wilted as we moved forward. It was so moist spiders could weave their webs in the very air and we had to walk wiping the webs and long, loose threads from our faces and hope no spider had fallen into our hair or down our blouses. It was the kind of humidity that made iguanas and lizards sleep with their eyes at half mast and even the insects were asleep. It was also the kind of heat that drove stray dogs down to the highways in search of water and their bloody carcasses marked the black asphalt from our mountain all the way to Acapulco.

It was so hot that at one point Maria and I sat down on some stones, after checking to see there was no scorpion or snake there, and rested for a minute.

A boy is never going to want to love me and that's that. I don't care, she said. I don't want anyone messing with my face. My mother said no boy will want to kiss me.

I tried to imagine the kiss, lips against her torn lips, a tongue inside of her torn mouth. I asked her if that meant she'd never have any children and she said her mother told her she would never get married or have children because no man would ever love her.

I don't want to be loved, Maria said, so who cares?

Maria, I don't want to be loved either. Who wants that? I think kissing sounds disgusting.

She turned and looked at me fiercely and I thought that she was going to spit on me or punch me but, at that moment, she fell in love with me.

Maria looked at me fiercely because everyone around here is fierce. In fact, all over Mexico it is known that the people who come from the state of Guerrero are full of anger and as dangerous as a white, transparent scorpion that's hidden in bed, under a pillow.

In Guerrero the heat, iguanas, spiders, and scorpions ruled. Life was not worth anything.

My mother used to say that all the time, Life is not worth anything. She also quoted the old famous song as if it were a prayer, If you're going to kill me tomorrow you might as well kill me today.

This was translated into all kinds of new versions of the same thing. I heard her tell my father once, If you're going to leave me tomorrow, you might as well leave me today.

I knew he would not come back. It was just as well because then she really would have done it. She would have cooked up a stew of fingernails, spit, and shredded hair. She would have mixed it with her menstrual blood and green chilies and chicken. She gave me the recipe. Not on a piece of paper, but she once told me about how to do it.

Always be the cook, she said. Never let anyone cook for you.

That stew of fingernails, spit, menstrual blood, and shredded hair would have tasted delicious. She was a good cook. It was for the best that he did not come back. She kept her machete sharp.

My mother said that she believed in revenge. It was a threat over my head, but it was also a lesson. I knew she was not going to forgive me for anything, but it also taught me not to forgive. She said that this was why she no longer went to church, even though she did have saints she loved, but she did not like all the forgiving business. I knew that much of her day was spent thinking about what she'd do to my father if he ever came back.

I watched my mother cut the tall grasses with her machete, or kill an iguana by breaking its head with a large stone, or scrape the thorns off a maguey pad, or kill a chicken by twisting its neck in her hands, and it was as if all the objects around her were my father's body. When she cut up a tomato I knew it was his heart she was slicing into thin wheels.

Once she leaned against the front door, pressed her body against the wood, and even that door became my father's back. The chairs were his lap. The spoons and forks were his hands.

One day Maria came running over to my house. We lived only a twenty-minute walk from each other by crossing land overgrown with rubber plants and short palm trees where large brown and green iguanas lay in the sun on flat rocks. They could swivel quickly and bite especially if you were an eight-year-old girl running and skipping past in red plastic flip-flops. She came alone, as she was the only girl allowed out because of her harelip. We all knew that no one would want her, not even if she was given away for nothing. People instantly recoiled when they looked at her. When I saw her at my front door, I knew something important had happened.

Ladydi, she cried, Ladydi!

My mother had gone to the market in Chilpancingo. At that young age our mothers still let us stay home alone if we promised not to go wandering off. As soon as the smallest bumps showed up on our chest, that was it. From that moment on, if we were to go out, steps were taken so that we did not look pretty.

Maria walked toward me with her arms splayed open at her sides and hugged me. It was strange to see her like that since she always had one hand covering her mouth. Maria moved with her left hand over half of her face, cupped across her mouth as if she was holding in a secret or about to spit out something.

What is it?

She stopped, out of breath and panting a little. She sat down beside me on the floor where I had been cutting out images from a magazine to paste in a copybook. This was one of my favorite pastimes.

The doctors are coming!

I didn't have to ask her anything. After eight years of waiting the famous doctors, the important expensive doctors from a hospital in Mexico City, they were coming to Chilpancingo to operate for free on children with deformities. Maria explained that the nurse from the clinic had appeared at their house about an hour after Maria had come home from school. She had drawn a sample of Maria's blood and taken her blood pressure to make sure she would be ready for the operation. They had to be at the clinic on Saturday at six in the morning.

That's in two days! I can't wait to tell Paula.

It occurred to me that Maria might think that after the operation she could be as beautiful as Paula. Even when I cut up old magazines, filled with the faces of movie stars and famous models, I knew none of them would stand a chance against Paula. Even though Paula's mother kept her hair short and even rubbed Paula's skin with chili powder so it would have a permanent red rash, Paula's beauty shone through anyway.

On Saturday morning my mother and I went down to the clinic to keep Maria's mother company. Estefani and her mother had also come down from their house.

Maria's brother, Mike, was there too. I realized I had not seen him for a while. He spent most of his time in Acapulco. At twelve he seemed grown up to me. He wore leather cuffs, like bracelets, on his wrists, which I'd never seen before, and he'd shaved his hair off.

Three army trucks were parked outside the clinic and twelve soldiers stood watch. These soldiers wore ski masks over their faces. They were also wearing aviator sunglasses over the eye openings in the wool. The backs of their necks glistened with sweat. The soldiers' machine guns were held ready as they surrounded the small rural health clinic.

On one of the trucks someone had tacked a sign that said: *Here doctors are operating on children.*

These measures were taken so that the drug traffickers wouldn't sweep down and kidnap the doctors and take them off. The drug traffickers kidnapped doctors for two reasons. Either they needed to have one of their own operated on, usually for bullet wounds, or they'd steal the Mexico City doctors for ransom. We knew that doctors would not come to our mountain unless they had protection.

We tried to get past the soldiers but they would not let us in the clinic so we had to wait at Ruth's beauty salon on the corner. We knew there was only one other child having an operation and this was a two-year-old boy who was born with an extra thumb. For two years this extra thumb was an important thing to talk about. Everyone had an opinion about it.

The truth was we knew the cause behind the deformities on our mountain. Everyone knew that the spraying of poisons to kill the crops of marijuana and poppies was harming our people.

In a fit of anger, the day before the operations, my mother said, Maria should just stay the way she is. And, thinking about that thumb boy, why don't they just cut his hand off too! Maybe then he'll stick around here when he grows up.

As we were standing outside the beauty salon we heard a far-off noise that was like a cattle stampede or an airplane flying too close to the ground. It only took a second for us to recognize that it was a convoy of SUVs.

The soldiers who guarded the clinic moved quickly and took cover behind their trucks.

We ran inside the salon and rushed to the back of the room as far from the windows as we could get. I dove under a sink.

Then the world was quiet and still. It seemed that even the dogs, birds, and insects stopped breathing.

No one said hush, hush, hush.

We expected bullets to start flying.

Every wall, window, and doorway on the main street, which was also the highway that ran through the town, was filled with holes. In our pockmarked world no one bothered filling up bullet holes or painting walls.

Twelve black SUVs drove past going at a great speed, way too fast, as if they were having a race. The windows were tinted black and the headlights were turned on even though it was daytime.

We could feel the whiz of speed and the ground shook around us. The large machines left a wake of dust and exhaust fumes behind and stirred up our minds with only one thought: Don't stop here.

Once the last SUV had passed there was a moment of

silence, of listening, before Ruth said, Okay, they're gone. So, who needs to get their hair done?

Ruth smiled and said she'd do everyone's nails for free while we waited to hear the outcome of the operations.

Ruth was a garbage baby. She must have been born from a big mistake. Why would someone throw their baby in the garbage like a banana peel or a rotten egg?

What's the damned difference between killing your baby and throwing it into the garbage, huh? my mother said.

I wondered if this question was a test.

There's a big difference, my mother said, answering her own question. At least a killing can be merciful.

Ruth was one of Mrs Silberstein's garbage babies. Mrs Silberstein was a Jewish woman from Los Angeles who had moved to Acapulco fifty years ago. When she'd heard the rumors about babies being thrown away in the trash, she spread the word out to all the garbage collectors in Acapulco, and let them know she would be willing to take care of the babies. In the past thirty years she'd raised at least forty children. One of these babies was Ruth.

Ruth was born from a black plastic garbage bag that was filled with dirty diapers, rotten orange peels, three empty beer bottles, a can of Coke, and a dead parrot wrapped in newspapers. Someone at the garbage dump heard cries coming out of the bag.

Ruth painted our nails and fed us potato chips right into our mouths so that the nail polish could dry without being smudged. She had trimmed my hair many times, but this was the first time I'd ever had my nails painted. It was the first act in my life that defined me as a girl.

Ruth held my hand gently in her hand as she painted the red enamel over each one of my oval, infant nails.

When she painted my thumb, I thought of the boy who was only one block away having his thumb removed.

Ruth blew on my hands to dry the polish.

You blow on them too, she said, so that they dry, and don't touch anything.

She swiveled away from me and took my mother's hand in hers.

What color, Rita?

The reddest color you have.

My hands were miraculously beautiful to me. I held them up to my face in the mirror.

What a world, my mother said. It's a nasty life.

Out the window, through glass shattered from bullets, we could watch the masked soldiers guarding the clinic. They were patting the dust off of their uniforms. The SUVs had created a small dust storm. I imagined what lay beyond the clinic's front door and had a vision of Maria lying on a white sheet, under a strong light bulb, surrounded by doctors and with her face cut in two pieces.

My mother's voice started up again behind me.

Sometimes I just think I'll grow the poppies too. Everyone else does, right? You're going to die no matter what so you might just as well die rich.

Oh, Rita!

Ruth spoke softly and slowly so when she said Rita it sounded like Reeetaaah. It made me happy to hear someone speak to my mother with such sweetness. Ruth's voice could heal and soothe.

What do you think? my mother asked.

The voices in the beauty parlor quieted down. We all wanted to hear what Ruth was going to answer. Everyone knew that Ruth was smarter and better than anyone else around here. She was also Jewish. Mrs Silberstein raised all her garbage orphans to be Jews.

Imagine, Ruth said. Imagine what it's like for me. I opened this beauty parlor fifteen years ago and what did I call it? I called it *The Illusion.* I called it this because my illusion, or my dream, was to do something. I wanted to make all of you pretty and surround myself with sweet smells.

Because Ruth was a garbage baby she could never get the smell of rotten oranges, the smell of someone's morning glass of juice, out of her mind.

Instead of making you pretty, what happened? Ruth asked.

Everyone looked down at their painted nails in silence.

What happened?

No one answered.

I have to make little girls look like boys, I have to make the older girls look plain, and I have to make pretty girls look ugly. This is an ugly parlor not a beauty parlor, Ruth said.

No one had an answer for this, not even my big-mouthed mother.

Maria's mother peered in the window of the beauty parlor. They've finished, she said through the shattered glass. Maria wants to see Ladydi, she said, pointing her finger at me.

You're not going anywhere until that nail polish is wiped off! my mother said.

Ruth pulled me toward her, sat me on her lap, and removed the nail polish. The acetone fumes filled my mouth and left a taste of lemon on my tongue.

In the small two-room clinic, the front room had been turned into an operating room. A nurse and two doctors were putting things away into suitcases while Maria lay on a cot under a window. From a bundle of white gauze bandages, her eyes peered out like small black stones. She looked at me with such intensity that I knew exactly what she was thinking. I'd known her all my life.

Her eyes said: Where is the boy? Did he have his thumb removed? Is he okay? What did they do with the thumb?

When I asked Maria's questions for her, the nurse answered that the boy had left an hour ago. The thumb was removed.

What happened to the thumb?

It will be incinerated, the nurse answered.

Burned?

Yes, burned.

Where?

Oh, we have it here on ice. We'll take it back to Mexico City and burn it there.

When I returned to the beauty parlor everyone's nail polish had been removed. It was clear that no one was going to risk going out into our world where men think they can steal you just because your nails are painted red.

As we walked home my mother asked me what Maria looked like. I said I couldn't see her because of the bandages but that the nurse said the operation had gone well.

Don't count on it, my mother said. She's going to have a scar.

We carefully crossed the highway that joined Mexico City and Acapulco and headed up the path to our small hut, which was shaded by an enormous banana tree.

As we walked a large iguana moved out from the underbrush and crossed our path. The movement made us look down at a long line of bright red ants marching toward the left of the path. We both stopped and looked around.

On the other side of the path there was another stream of ants going in the same direction.

Something's dead, my mother said.

She looked up. There were five vultures circling above us in the air. The birds flew around and around, dipping down close to the earth and rising up again. The smell of death was in their wings.

The birds continued to soar above us as we reached our house.

Once inside my mother walked to the kitchen and took out four little bottles of nail polish from inside her sleeve. She placed a red bottle and three pink bottles on the kitchen table.

You stole nail polish from Ruth?

I didn't know why I was surprised. Anytime we went anywhere my mother stole something. I just could not believe that she would steal from Ruth.

Shut up and go and do your homework, my mother said.

I don't have any homework.

Then just shut up, my mother said. Go and wash your hands so you can get them dirty again.

My mother walked over to the window and looked up at the sky.

It's a dog, she said. Those are just too many damn vultures for it to be a dead mouse.

Three

We lived off my mother's wages as a cleaning lady. Every Friday after school my mother and I walked down to the highway and waited for a bus to take us an hour's drive to the port. She had no one to leave me with at home. Everywhere she went I had to go too.

Before the Reyes family arrived from Mexico City, my mother had to mop the house, make the beds, and put insecticide everywhere in order to kill ants, spiders, and especially scorpions.

When I was a child, she let me be in charge of the insecticide, which came in a spray bottle. As my mother cleaned, I sprayed the insecticide in corners, under the beds, inside closets, and around the sinks in the bathrooms. It made my mouth taste strange for days, as if I'd sucked on a piece of copper wire.

We had a servant's room behind the garage. My mother used to tie me to the bed with a rope. She did this so that she could get her work done and not worry that I might wander off and fall into the swimming pool. She'd tie me to the bed for hours with a loaf of white bread, a glass of milk, and some crayons and paper.

Sometimes she would bring me books to look at from

the house. These books were usually architecture books on the world's great mansions, or books on museums.

Of course my mother also stole from the Reyes family. On our way back home on Sunday night I'd see what she'd taken. As the bus hurtled over the burning asphalt toward a land of red insects and women, she'd slowly take things from pockets and look them over.

In the darkness of the bus I watched as tweezers came out of her blouse and three long red candles were removed from her sleeve.

One night as the lights from cars coming in the opposite direction lit up the inside of the vehicle, my mother handed me a small bag of chocolate eggs.

Here, I took these for you, she said.

I ate them in the bus as I looked out the window and into the dense jungle that lined the side of the highway.

After Maria had her harelip operation everything changed. If it had not been for Maria, we might not have noticed the vultures circling above our house as we walked back from the clinic.

I'm going to go and investigate what's dead, my mother said, moving away from the window where she was looking out at the sky.

You stay here, she said.

I waited for about an hour listening to music on my iPod, which she'd also stolen from the Reyes family, before she came back.

She looked worried and she'd been pulling at her hair on the left side of her head. It was sticking out in a great frizzy clump. I pulled the earbuds, and the sound of Daddy Yankee, out of my ears.

Ladydi, listen, she said. There's a dead man out there and we have to bury him.

What do you mean?

There's a damn corpse out there.

Who is it?

He's naked.

Naked?

You're going to have to close your eyes and help me put him in the ground. Go get some spoons, the big one, and get out of those clothes, I'm going for the spade out back.

I stood up and took off the clean clothes I'd worn to go to the clinic in the morning and changed into an old pair of jeans and a T-shirt.

My mother returned with the spade that we usually used for digging up anthills.

Okay, she said. Follow me.

I followed my mother. I counted five vultures above us. My mother made a breathless sound, like panting, as we walked. We reached the corpse in a few minutes.

This is too close to the house, I said.

This is too damn close to the house. You're right.

Yes.

He was dumped here.

Who is he?

Does he look familiar to you?

No.

In this land one can go out for a walk and find a huge iguana, a papaya tree covered with dozens of large fruits, an enormous anthill, marijuana plants, poppies, or a corpse.

It was the body of a young boy. He looked about sixteen years old. He was lying on his back looking up into the sun.

Poor thing, my mother said.

The sun will burn his face.

Yes.

His hands had been cut off and white and blue veins threaded out from his bloody wrists into the dirt like bloated worms.

The letter P was carved into his forehead.

There was a note pinned to his shirt with a large safety pin with a pink plastic clasp. It was the kind of pin used for diapers.

Does that note say what I think it says? my mother asked as she began to dig. Does that say: *Paula and two girls*?

Yes, that's what it says.

You, get over here! Start digging. We need to hurry.

As the vultures circled above us we dug using the spade, the large spoon, and our hands.

Deeper, deeper, my mother said. We need to dig deeper or the animals will pull him out in the night.

We dug for over two hours and the ground produced transparent worms, green beetles, and pink stones.

My mother scraped at the earth and looked over her shoulder every so often in a panic. I feel eyes are on us, she whispered.

Wouldn't it have been better to just let the jungle take care of the body? I asked. But even as I said this, I knew the answer.

The police and drug traffickers kept an eye out for vultures. My mother said that the birds were the best informants around. She did not want anyone to come snooping around, looking at her daughter.

After the hole was deep enough we pulled the body into the hole and covered it over with dirt.

I looked at my hands. The dirt had been pushed way

deep under my nails and no washing was going to get it out. Not for weeks.

When we finished my mother said, I never thought you were born to bury a dead boy with me. That was not in the prediction of my life.

Once, when my mother was about twenty years old, she went to Acapulco and paid a fortuneteller to tell her about what was going to happen in her life. This was a fortuneteller who had a small space that she rented between two bars on the main street in Acapulco. My mother told me that she'd been attracted to the woman's sign, which said: *You are only unfortunate if you don't know your fortune.*

My mother used to watch tourists from all over the world pay money to hear what this woman said. She knew she had to go. It took my mother years to get up the courage to go inside and pay to have her fortune told.

I was just an Indian from the countryside, my mother said. But that woman kissed my money and whispered to me, Money has no country or race. Once the money is in my pocket I don't know who gave it to me.

My mother always brought up this experience. That fortuneteller predicted nothing. Anything that happened to my mother was always punctuated with the words: This was not a prediction in my life. As the years went by the disappointment grew deeper as my mother realized that nothing the woman said had come true.

Mark my words, Ladydi, my mother said. One of these weekends when we're in Acapulco we're going to go and find that fortuneteller and I'm going to tell her to give my money back.

After the last pile of dirt had been thrown over the dead boy's body my mother said, Let's say a prayer.

You say it, I answered.

Get on our knees, my mother said. This is serious.

We both knelt on the white worms, the beetles, and pink stones.

On the happy day that Maria had her mouth fixed and the little baby had his extra thumb removed, this young boy appeared. We pray for rain. Amen.

Then we stood up and walked back to our house.

As we washed our hands in the kitchen sink, my mother said, Yes, Ladydi, I'm going to tell Paula's mother. I have to. She needs to know.

My mother stood at the kitchen sink. She took out the note that had been pinned on the corpse from her pocket and lit a match to the paper. Paula's name turned to ash.

Paula never knew her father. To think that there was a man out there someplace who did not know he'd sired the most beautiful girl in Mexico!

Paula's mother, Concha, never told anyone who Paula's father was but my mother had her own theory. Concha used to work as a bedroom maid at the house of a rich family in Acapulco.

On the day Concha was fired, she came back to the mountain with two things: a baby in her belly and a wad of pesos in her hand.

There's nothing worse than a fatherless daughter, my mother said. The world just eats those girls alive.

After we'd washed, my mother and I went over to Paula's house, which was a short walk down to the edge of the highway.

I sat with Paula while my mother spoke to Concha about the corpse. At eleven, Paula was still thin and stringy, but her beauty was there. Everyone turned and stared at her wherever she went. Everyone could see what was coming.

After this visit, my mother and I walked to the highway

and the store that stayed open late beside the gas station. She bought a six-pack of beer. This was the day that she stopped eating and only drank beer.

What did Paula's mother say? I asked.

Not much.

Was she scared?

To death. She'll be dead in the morning.

What do you mean?

I don't know. Those words just came out of me.

The next morning my mother was still asleep when I left for school. I looked at her face. There was no mirror there.

Four

We never told anyone about the field of poppies.

We found the poppy crop a year before Maria's harelip operation. I remember because Maria covered her mouth on that day when she said, I am afraid of flowers.

One day Estefani, Paula, Maria, and I decided to go for a walk. This was misbehaviour, as we were never allowed to wander off and go for walks by ourselves. We left from Estefani's house on a Saturday afternoon.

Estefani's family had a real house. They had three bedrooms, a kitchen, and a living room. Estefani lived with her mother, Augusta, and two little sisters, Manuela and Dolores. On our mountain only Estefani's father came back to Mexico from the United States every year. He also sent them money every month. Thanks to him there was electricity on our mountain as he'd paid someone a lot of money to get that done. Estefani's father worked as a gardener in Florida. We also knew that he'd once worked in Alaska on fishing boats. In Florida, Americans hired him most of the time, but he also worked for rich Mexicans who had fled from the violence. He said that many of these Mexicans were victims of kidnappings.

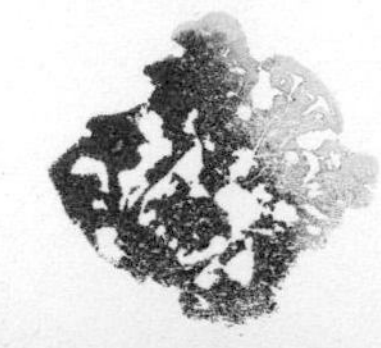

Estefani had many toys from the United States. She had a fairy watch that lit up in the dark and a plastic doll that spoke and the lips even moved.

In their kitchen there was a microwave oven, a toaster, and an electrical juicer. The entire house was fitted with ceiling lights. They all had electrical toothbrushes.

Estefani's house was one of my mother's favorite topics of conversation. After my mother had guzzled her third beer, I knew she would only talk about Estefani's house or my father.

Their damn sheets match their bedspreads and their towels match the round rug on the floor. Have you seen how their dishes match their napkins? she said. In the United States everything has to match!

I had to admit she was right. Even the three sisters were always dressed in matching clothes.

Look at this dirt floor, she said. look at it! Your father did not even love us enough to buy a bag of cement. He wanted us to walk with the spiders and walk with the ants. If a scorpion bites you and kills you, it will be your father's fault.

Everything was his fault. If it rained, he'd built a roof that leaked. If it was hot, he'd built the house too far from the rubber trees. If my grades were poor at school, I was his daughter, as stupid as he was. If I broke something like a water glass, I was as clumsy as he was. If I talked too much, I was exactly like him, I never shut up. If I was quiet, I was just like him, I thought I was better than everyone else.

One day, when Estefani's mother had a cold and had locked herself up in her room, Maria, Paula, Estefani, and I decided to go for a walk.

Let's go exploring, Maria said. Her voice was muffled

back then because her hand was always covering her mouth and the exposed red flesh from her harelip.

Let's walk in the direction of Mexico City, Paula said. She was always thinking about going to Mexico City. It was the one place we could all find instantly when we looked at a map of Mexico. Our index fingers could point it out right in the middle of the country. If Mexico were a body, Mexico City would be its navel.

We walked in a straight line away from Estefani's house, through the iguana paths that took us deeper into the jungle overgrowth. I was at the back. Maria walked at the front, holding one hand over her mouth. Paula looked beautiful even though her mother had blackened her teeth with a black marker which had bled everywhere so even her lips were black. Estefani walked in front of me in a matching set of a pink T-shirt and shorts. She was already so tall she looked years older than the rest of us. Looking at my friends, it made me wonder, What about me? What did I look like?

You look just like your father, my mother said. You have brown-red skin, brown hair, brown eyes, and white teeth. (A teacher had once told us that the people of Guerrero were Afro-Indian.)

As Maria, Paula, Estefani, and I walked in the direction of Mexico City, climbing higher than our homes and up from the highway, we slowly felt the jungle lose its density and the sun began to burn the tops of our heads. We walked and looked down at our feet as we moved. We did not want to step on a snake or some poisonous creature.

As soon as I can I am going to leave this horrible jungle, Paula said.

The rest of us knew that if there were anyone who could, it would be Paula with her TV commercial face.

As if we'd crossed a border, from one minute to the next, we'd left our hothouse jungle world and reached a clearing. The sun was strong. We stood before the brilliance of lavender and black as a huge field, a bonfire of poppies appeared before us.

The place seemed to be deserted except for a downed army helicopter, a mangled mess of metal skids and blades among the poppies.

The field of flowers smelled like gasoline.

Maria's hand slipped into mine. I did not need to turn and look at her to know it was her small, cool hand like an apple peel. We would recognize each other in the dark and even in a dream.

Nobody had to say, Be quiet, or, Hush, or Let's get out of here.

When we got back to Estefani's house, her mother was still asleep. The four of us went into Estefani's bedroom and closed the door.

We all knew the sound of the army helicopters approaching from far away. We also knew the smell of Paraquat mixed with the scent of papaya and apples.

My mother said, Those crooks are paid, paid by the drug traffickers, not to drop that damn Paraquat on the poppies and so they drop it wherever else on the mountain, on us!

We also knew that the poppy growers strung wires above the crops in order to down the helicopters or, in some cases, simply shot them down with their rifles and AK-47s. Those army helicopters had to go back to their bases and report that they had dropped the herbicide so they dropped it anywhere they could. They did not want to get near the fields where they would be shot down for sure. When the helicopters came by and got rid of the stuff over our houses we could smell the ammonia scent in everything and our eyes burned for days. My mother said this was the reason she could never stop coughing.

My body, she said, is the army's damn poppy field.

In Estefani's room we all promised that this would be our secret.

Maria and I already had a secret. It had to do with her older brother Mike. He had a gun.

My mother always said that Mike was a piece of shit who had been placed on this earth to break a woman's heart in pieces. She said she'd known this ever since he was born.

Maria was born with all the bad luck God had to give on that day, my mother said. God even gave her a brother who does not deserve to be a brother to anyone.

Mike told us he found the gun down by the highway in a large, black plastic garbage bag that had burst open. The gun was there, the metal shining, among broken eggshells. It still had two bullets.

I believed him. I knew you could find anything in garbage bags.

Five

My father could pick up a snake by the tail and twist it in two parts as if he was tearing a piece of chewing gum. His piercing whistle made the iguanas scurry away from the jungle paths. He was always singing about something.

Why talk if you can sing? he said.

He always had a cigarette between two fingers, a beer in one hand, and a straw hat with a short brim on his head. He hated to wear a baseball cap like everyone else.

Every morning he'd walk down to the highway and take the cheap bus to Acapulco where he worked in the daytime as a poolside bartender. This was at the Acapulco Bay Hotel. My mother would place a clean and ironed shirt and pair of pants in a plastic supermarket bag, which were the clothes he would change into when he got to work.

During the course of the day, I used to watch my mother. As the hours went by she became more and more excited. By eight o'clock she knew that the bus had left him down on the road and that he was walking up the mountain toward us. I watched her put on some lipstick and change into a clean dress. We could hear him approach before we saw him because he'd be singing and his voice came to us through the dark banana and papaya trees.

When he finally stood at the door, he'd close his eyes and open his arms. Who do I get to hug first? he asked. It was always my mother. She'd step down hard on my foot, push me back, or even trip me before she'd let me get to him first.

He would sit in our little side room off the kitchen, which was like a kind of living room where we could be inside away from the mosquitoes, and tell us about his day serving drinks and Cokes to tourists from the United States and Europe. Once in a while he served soap-opera stars or politicians. These stories were the most interesting to us.

As the years passed my mother grew angrier and began to drink too much. I remember this was almost a year after Maria's harelip operation. One night she talked too much.

Your father has slept with Paula's mother, Concha, and with Estefani's mother, and everyone around here. Yes, he did it with every single one of my friends, every single one. And let me tell you whom he has been doing it to these days. It's been Ruth, she said.

My mother picked up another bottle of beer and drank back a great long swig. Her eyes seemed almost cross-eyed to me.

So, Ladydi, she continued, you might as well know the truth about your sweet loving daddy. All of it.

Please, Mama. Stop.

Don't ever say your mother didn't tell you the truth.

And then she burst into tears, hundreds of tears. My mother became a huge rainstorm.

And you might as well know the whole truth, she sobbed.

I don't want to know anymore, I said.

Maria's mother too. He slept with Maria's mother too

and, listen to me, that was the curse. I told your father that Maria's harelip, that rabbit face, hare's face, was God's punishment.

I became very still, still like when a white, almost transparent scorpion is on the wall above your bed. Still like when you see a snake curled up behind the coffee tin. Still like waiting for the helicopter to dump the burning herbicide all over your body as you run home from school. Still like when you hear an SUV turning off the highway and it almost sounds like a lion, even though you've never heard a lion.

What exactly are you saying, Mama?

Oh my God, my mother said, holding her hand over her mouth.

She seemed to spit the words into the palm of her hand as if they were olive pits or a plum seed or a piece of tough meat she couldn't swallow. It was as if she tried to catch the words in her hand before they came out into the room and traveled into me.

When the words came into me it was as if they traveled from a coiled spring. My body was a pinball machine and the words hit like metal balls banging and rushing down and up my arms and legs and around my neck until they fell into the prized hole of my heart.

Don't look at me like that, Ladydi, my mother said. Hey, and don't act all high and mighty like you didn't know any of this gossip.

But she knew perfectly well I didn't know anything about my father's ways, or not these ways. What she did know, because she was a drunk and not a fool, was that she'd just killed my daddy for me. She might as well have shot a bullet through his Daddy-loves-only-me heart.

My reaction was to say, Give me a beer and don't tell me I'm too young.

You're eleven.

No, I'm twelve.

No, you're eleven.

She opened and passed a bottle of beer over to me. I drank it down fast just the way she did. The way I'd seen her do it hundreds of times. And that was the first time I got drunk. I quickly learned that all it takes is some alcohol to solve everything. When you're drunk you don't care if a battalion of mosquitoes bites your arms up or a scorpion stings your hand or if your father is a lying bastard and your best friend, with a broken face, turns out to be your half-sister.

Now I understood why my mother always liked to say how she had marched over to look at Maria after she was born. It was to see if that baby looked like my father, which of course she did. Maria looks exactly like my father and maybe this is also why Maria's father left. Maybe it wasn't the harelip that scared him after all. Maybe he thought he was not going to spend the rest of his life feeding the face of his wife's lover's baby.

When my daddy came home from work that night, full of songs, he found his wife and daughter passed out drunk.

The next morning I woke up to find my mother sitting on the kitchen stool by the window. I guess he took one look at us and, later that night, listened to my mother rant about what she'd told me and why. She must have said, Do you think we were going to lie to her forever? You think you're Frank Sinatra out there in Acapulco serving people margaritas with those silly little plastic umbrellas.

I had a large collection of those colorful cocktail paper umbrellas, which my father had brought back for me over the years. He also brought me glow-in-the-dark cocktail stirring sticks. He helped me paste these all around my bed so that I could watch them glow in the night. He also gave me dollar bills every now and again, which were given to him by tourists from the USA. I'd saved up thirty dollars. I kept this money in an Archie comic book in my bedroom.

Knowing that Maria was my half-sister also made me feel differently about Mike. It gave me sisterly feelings toward him. From then on, I always bought him a birthday present.

Shortly after this, my father went to the United States to look for work. He only came back a few more times and then he was gone for good. All we had to remember him by was the satellite dish attached to the tallest palm tree on our small plot of land and a large flat-screen television and, of course, Maria.

I should be skinned in a butcher's shop and hanging from a hook, my mother said.

That was the first time my daddy left. He didn't even wake me up from my drunk, new-drunk sleep to say goodbye.

He didn't say goodbye to you because he couldn't look you in the eye! Frank Sinatra just slunk out of here like an old street dog that's ashamed to be a dog, my mother said.

She let every one of our friends know that he'd left home without even saying goodbye to his daughter.

Two months later we heard from the USA to Mexico rumor mill that he'd gone to the border and managed to get across the river in Tijuana, at the San Ysidro port of entry, hidden in the back of a truck under a false floor between the wheels and the bumper. Then he went down Interstate 5 and into the United States.

It got back to us that the minute he crossed the border and was heading deep into the state of Texas, he had started to sing songs, one after another. This was all the proof my mother and I need in order to confirm that these rumors were true.

After my father crossed the border he went to Florida where he was working as a gardener. This made my mother spit on the ground and say, A gardener! That lying son of a bitch does not know anything about gardening.

We both tried to imagine him carrying a spade or a rake and planting roses. He could seduce and sweet-talk himself into anything.

When he finally wired us some money, about three months after he'd left, my mother was speechless. It took me a while to figure out what had slapped the words out of her mouth and left her empty. The money my father had wired did not come from one of those glamorous-sounding places in Florida like Miami, Orlando, or Palm Beach but from a town called Boca Raton. This was just too much for my mother.

She said, He left this place to go to the Rat's Mouth?

Six

The following school year we had a teacher called José Rosa, from Mexico City. He was doing his social service and had been sent to teach at our school. We tried not to become too attached to these strangers who came and went, but sometimes it was hard.

José Rosa was a handsome twenty-three-year-old man who was sent to our world of women.

Paula, Estefani, Maria, and I watched as our mothers fell in love with this young teacher. Every morning our mothers sent him treats in our lunch bags or just hung out around the school.

This was also the time when Paula, Maria, Estefani, and I first protested against being made unattractive or dressing like boys. We wanted José Rosa's eyes to look at us as women.

The only person who resisted him was Estefani. She was the first person who saw him walking up the path to our one-room school in the jungle under the dying orange tree. She saw him walk his city-walk in his city clothes and haircut and then she heard him talk his city-talk.

Who's going to get his city-kiss? Who is going to get his skyscraper-kiss? Estefani asked.

Estefani was the only one who had been to Mexico City. In fact, she'd been to Mexico City many times. Her mother was sick and they had to go and see a doctor every few months. Estefani's mother had almost died. We were all very worried about this because Estefani was only nine at the time. Estefani's father had left to go and work in the United States on the fishing boats in Alaska and was not around to help. Estefani said that her mother just kept getting skinnier and no matter how hard she tried to gain weight, she couldn't. Her mother's dark skin began to turn a silvery color.

But the truth of the story was that Estefani's father did not bring back the smell and taste of Alaskan king salmon, rainbow trout, or Arctic char. He did not bring back a bag of pine needles or photographs of grizzly bears or an eagle feather. He brought back the AIDS virus, which he gave to Estefani's mother, like giving her a rose or a box of chocolates.

In Chilpancingo, next to the canteen that had so many bullet holes in its door the dark bar could be looked at through the round wounds, there was a clinic where for twenty pesos you could get an AIDS test. The men came and went to the United States and the women, year after year, walked down past the canteen for an AIDS test. There were some who did not want to know. Those women prayed.

When Estefani's mother was diagnosed with AIDS, her husband left. He slapped her across the face three times back and forth and back again and called her a whore. He said if she had AIDS it was because she'd been unfaithful. We all knew this was impossible. There were no men on our mountain.

After this, Estefani's house, which we had so admired,

began to fall to pieces. The appliances stopped working, but Estefani's mother still kept them. The toys broke. The matching towels and rugs frayed.

Estefani boasted that she'd seen many city men, because she'd gone to Mexico City with her mother, and so she was not at all impressed with our new teacher. In fact, she used to say that our teacher, José Rosa, was not as handsome as other men she'd seen.

When José Rosa walked into our schoolroom one hot August morning we could still smell the city surrounding him. His odor was of cars, exhaust fumes, and cement. He was very pale.

He looks like a glass of milk, Maria said.

No, like a movie star, Paula said.

No, Estefani disagreed. He looks like a worm.

He introduced himself to each one of us and shook our hands. His hand in my hand still belonged to the city. It felt cool and dry. It had not peeled a mango or torn into a papaya. He also wore a straw hat. Later he told us it was a panama hat, which we thought was elegant. Other than my father, he was the first man we'd ever seen who did not wear a baseball cap. José Rosa had very curly black hair and light brown eyes with long eyelashes that curled upward toward his eyebrows.

When my mother saw him she said, Well, Ladydi, we'd better start digging a hole for him too!

On the first day of school, we'd arrived with our mothers to register and officially meet the new teacher. This was a routine that we followed at the beginning of the school year. On that first day we just looked like ourselves. We were messy and born from the jungle so we were like the relatives of papaya trees, iguanas, and butterflies.

After having seen José Rosa in his straw hat, there was

a massive rush to Ruth's beauty salon. We watched as our mothers had their hair washed and trimmed. The mothers who had curly hair wanted straight hair and those with straight hair wanted curly hair. It was only my mother who insisted that she wanted her black hair colored blond. Ruth was pleased because she was always trying to get everyone to change their hair color.

We watched Ruth fix up our mothers as we spun around and around in the hair-salon chairs or watched the huge passenger buses pass by from the beauty parlor's bullet-riddled window. We longed to have our hair done and our nails painted, but we were not allowed.

When Ruth took the towel off my mother's wet hair, her black frizz had been transformed into yellow frizz. There was a sudden quiet in the beauty salon as we stared at her yellow cotton-candy hair.

On the second day of school everyone looked like they were dressed for Christmas. Our mothers' brown faces were covered with makeup and lipstick. Estefani's mother was even wearing false eyelashes, which looked like antennas coming out of her worn, sickly face.

When José Rosa arrived it was as if a large mirror had fallen into the jungle. When we looked at him, we looked at ourselves. Every imperfection, our skin, scars, things we had never even noticed, we saw in him.

My mother was the first one to invite him over for dinner. He's not going to believe it when he sees I know about grammar. I know about onomatopoeia and verbs, she said. I do, right?

She spent the day sweeping our dirt floor and cleaning the dust off of everything. Ever since my father had left, she'd never done any housecleaning.

I could understand why my father left our home, the

jungle, and my mother (even though she wasn't yet the angry drunk she became), but I could never understand how he could have left me.

When José Rosa came to our clean house, we sat outside, under the papaya tree; my mother and José drank beer and I drank a Coke. When my mother handed José Rosa the bottle of beer, she did not hand him a glass. In Guerrero we all drink straight out of bottles.

José spent his visit with us complaining about our mountain. He didn't understand why we never used drinking glasses or why we had houses, but almost always slept outside at night. We listened quietly as he complained that everyone had appliances like televisions, satellite antennas, and washing machines, but that we had no furniture and still lived on dirt floors.

José Rosa discussed the way we had our light wired in, which was actually illegal since we took it from the light posts down on the highway, and threaded the wires up along the paths and through the trees. He could not understand why we ate beef so often and so few fruits and vegetables. He went on and on. José Rosa even said that the large toads near the school were the ugliest things he'd ever seen. He could not stand the enormous black ants that had taken over his small house and, of course, the heat was unbearable.

My now blond mother listened to all this as she drank one beer after another. Her makeup seemed to slip off her face from the sweat and melt down onto her neck. By the time her lipstick had stained the opening of five beer bottles and José Rosa expressed that he had to wear socks even in this heat since, after all, he'd been raised to wear socks, she was upset.

And then he said it.

He said, How can you all live like this, in a world without any men? How?

My mother took in a breath. It seemed that even the ants on the ground stopped moving. José Rosa's question stood in the hot wet air, as if spoken words could be suspended. I could reach out and touch the letter H and O and W.

Do you ever watch television, Mr Rosa? my mother asked in that too-slow tone of hers that she'd get into when she was angry.

She placed her empty beer bottle on the ground beside her.

I counted six empty beer bottles on the ground beside her. Big black ants were already going in and out of some of the bottles.

You men don't get it, yet, do you? she said. This is a land of women. Mcxico belongs to women. If you've watched any television then you've seen that show about the Amazon.

The river? José Rosa asked.

She told him about the female warriors and how the word Amazon means without breast.

My mother had television-knowledge. That's what she called it.

No, no, I don't know this story, José Rosa said.

You have to watch the History Channel, Mr Teacher. We always watch the History Channel, right, Ladydi?

José Rosa did not want to talk about the Greeks or to let it be known that he did not know anything about the Amazons.

Yes, that's interesting, but where are the men? he asked. Do you know where they all are exactly?

Oh yes, we know. They're not here.

My mother stood up and walked into our two-room house. She didn't really walk but slithered with her feet slipping too far forward in her plastic flip-flops so that her toes curled over the front of the sandals like talons.

Wait here, don't move, she said and disappeared into the black shade of our hot, raw cement home.

This was the first time that José Rosa and I were alone. He looked at me kindly and asked in his city-voice, which always sounded exotic to me, does she always drink so much?

I knew my mother had gone inside and passed out from the beer and heat. I could tell from her walk that her blond frizzy mass of hair was now pressed down into the pillow on a small cot in a corner and that she would not wake up until late that night.

Come with me, I said. I want to show you something.

We both stood and my teacher followed me around the small house to the back.

There, I said, look. This is the beer-bottle cemetery.

José Rosa stood still and breathless at the sight of my mother's mound of hundreds and hundreds of brown-glass bottles dumped in piles and lying under swarms of bees.

To the right of the beer cemetery was our laundry line that was tied between two papaya trees. My mother had cleaned the house but she'd forgotten to take the clothes off the line. José Rosa looked at our yellow and pink underwear hanging limp in the windless air. These panties were filled with holes and the crotch on some was brown and worn thin from my mother overscrubbing her menstrual bloodstains.

How old are you exactly? José Rosa asked me as we turned and walked back around the house. He used words such as *exactly* and *quite,* and they seem like well-mannered, proper city words.

I'd better go now, he said.

Everyone wanted to leave once my mother had had too much to drink. I was used to it.

Yes. She's asleep now. I'll walk you down to the highway.

He was relieved to have me walk with him. I knew that city people were frightened by the jungle and he seemed more frightened than most.

Why did you come here? I asked as we walked down our steep hill toward the highway. He lived in a small room above Ruth's beauty parlor.

I watched him as he moved trying to avoid stepping on the big red ants in his black leather lace-up city shoes. He looked down at his feet and up to the trees, back and forth. As the day turned to dusk dozens of mosquitoes lit on his neck and arms. He tried to wave them away. The jungle knew this city man was among us.

At the highway I told him I was not allowed to cross and had to go back home.

You know not to go out at night, right? I said. Someone did tell you this?

The night belongs to the drug traffickers, the army, and the police just like it belongs to the scorpions, I said.

José Rosa nodded his head.

No matter what, you don't leave your house, not even if you hear the sound of gunfire or someone screaming for help, okay?

Thank you, he said as he took my hand and leaned over and kissed my cheek.

No one in the jungle holds anyone's hand or kisses anyone's cheek. This is a city custom, or a custom that can only exist in a cool climate. In our hot land touching is just more heat.

When I returned to my house my mother was still passed out. It took me a few seconds to recognize her form in the bed. I'd forgotten that she'd bleached her hair. The blond mop covered her small pillow.

My mother's hands were lying across her stomach. As I approached I could see she was holding something shiny gripped between her fingers.

The next morning my mother seemed upset. She would not even look at me.

So when did José Rosa leave? I didn't notice when he left, she said.

You just passed out, Mother. What were you thinking? He's my teacher!

My mother paced and pulled at her bleached blond hair. I didn't know if she was angry or sad.

Finally she said, I was just turning inside out, turning inside out so that my bones were on the outside and my heart was hanging here in the middle of my chest like a medallion. It was just too much and so I had to lie down. Ladydi, I knew that man could see my liver and my spleen. He could've just leaned over and plucked my eye off of my face like a grape.

What are you doing with a gun, Mama?

My mother stopped and was quiet for a moment.

What gun?

What are you doing with a gun, Mama?

Some men need killing, my mother answered.

I sat down beside her and began to rub her back gently.

I have to go to school now, Mama, or I'm going to be late, I said.

Why the hell can't this place have a bar full of men so that you can get drunk and get yourself kissed?

I'm going to school by myself. I have to go, Mama.

I left her there on the floor and walked out of the house.

As I moved down the hill an army of ants was marching in several lines down the mountain toward the highway. Lizards were moving in the same direction, moving very quickly. The birds above me were also disturbed and flying away.

That morning everything on the mountain seemed to be pushing down toward the black asphalt river.

And then I knew why.

Way off, far off, I heard a helicopter.

I ran toward the school as fast as I could.

At the schoolroom everyone was already inside and the small door was closed.

Let me in, I cried.

José Rosa opened the door. I pushed past him and ran over to Maria and Estefani who stood at the window looking up.

Where's Paula? I asked.

My friends shook their heads.

José Rosa was confused and bewildered. Maria explained that the helicopter meant the army was coming to dump Paraquat on the poppy fields.

Everyone is running for cover, she explained. You never know where the herbicide might be sprayed.

We could hear the helicopter getting closer until it finally passed over our little one-room school and moved away.

Do you smell anything? Estefani asked.

I don't, Maria said. No.

José Rosa sat down and took out a small box of white chalk from his leather briefcase and walked toward the blackboard. He wrote out four columns with the subject headings History, Geography, Mathematics, and Spanish Language.

We took out our copybooks and pencils from our school satchels and began to copy down what José Rosa had written.

As I wrote the word History I could smell it. By the time I'd written the words Spanish Language there was no doubt in my mind that I was smelling Paraquat.

The three of us knew it. José Rosa did not.

We also felt the absence of Paula.

As the scent grew stronger we could sense the poison creep in under the schoolroom door.

At the moment when Maria squirmed and was about to stand and insist that we had to get out of that room, Paula pushed open the door and entered panting and crying.

She was drenched in the poison.

Paula was crying with her eyes closed and her lips pressed firmly together.

We all knew that if you got any Paraquat in your mouth you could die.

In her race to outrun the helicopter she'd lost her flip-flops and her satchel. Her dress was drenched and her hair dripped with the stinging liquid. Paula kept her eyes firmly shut. The herbicide can blind you too. It burns everything.

Maria was the first to jump up out of her chair.

In order not to touch her, Maria guided her by pushing Paula with her notebook into the small bathroom built at the back.

Estefani and I followed them. In the bathroom Paula tore off her dress. We tried to clean her off with tap water, but it came out much too slowly, so we also scooped water out from the toilet bowl. We washed her eyes and mouth over and over again.

I could taste the poison. Where some had rubbed onto my skin, I could feel the burning, which could turn a radiant poppy into a piece of tar the size of a raisin.

José Rosa watched in silence. He peered into the room from outside, and covered his mouth and nose with his arm, holding the white cotton shirtsleeve against his face.

We washed off the poison, but we knew much of it was inside her already. Paula did not speak or cry, as she stood naked and trembling in the small bathroom.

It was Estefani who had the idea of wrapping her up in the frayed cloth curtain that hung in the schoolroom.

We walked her through the jungle, down to the highway, and back up to her house. Even though we offered her our own plastic flip-flops, Paula said no and limped on her bare feet. She was afraid there might be Paraquat in the grass along the path to her house and we would be burnt by it.

We handed Paula over to her mother who could only say, It was only a matter of time.

We knew she would not be able to reach a sponge into Paula's body, as if she were a bottle, and wash the poison out.

At home my mother was sitting on the ground at the back of the house overlooking the beer cemetery. Her hair stood up in the air like a yellow halo. The brown-glass bottles and silver cans gleamed and shone under the late-morning sun.

I sat down beside her.

She turned and looked at me and then looked up at the sun and said, What are you doing here so early, huh?

I was still shivering.

Oh my, Ladydi, she said. What happened?

She leaned toward me and placed her arm around me. I told her the whole story.

Daughter, my child, this is, of course, an omen. We have been distinguished. The worm will turn, she said.

She was right. Later, when Paula was stolen, I knew this day had been an omen. She was the first to be chosen.

That night Estefani, Maria, Paula, and I menstruated for the first time. My mother said it was because of the full moon. Estefani's mother said it was because of the poison triggering something bad inside of us.

But we knew what had really happened.

José Rosa had seen Paula naked. He saw her dark skin and her breasts with their large, brown areolae and soft, black-red nipples and the black hair between her legs. He saw her young, teenage beauty. At that moment, we became one woman and it was as if he'd seen us all.

Seven

I promised my mother that I would never tell Maria that she was my half-sister.

I don't want to shake the leaves out of the trees, my mother said.

I won't tell her.

As Maria grew and the scar from her harelip faded, she looked exactly like my father. If he'd seen her, he would have thought he was looking in a mirror.

My mother noticed it too. She would stare at Maria in a quiet way, studying her face. She was struggling between wanting to take Maria into her arms and kiss her and wanting to slap her hard across the face.

I loved Maria. Out of everyone in that godforsaken-godforgotten-hottest-hell-on-earth place, as my mother liked to call our mountain, she was the kindest person of all. She would walk around a big red fire ant before she'd step on one.

The year that José Rosa was our teacher I remember as a series of events.

The first event was the day of his arrival, combined with the visit at my house when I showed him our beer cemetery. The second event that stands out is the day that Paula was rained on with herbicide.

That year was also measured by watching my mother's blond hair grow out. By the time the school year was over, her black roots reached almost to her ears. She never dyed it over black, touched it up blond again, or even trimmed it, because Ruth's beauty salon had closed. And this, the closing of Ruth's salon, was the third event of that year.

No one saw a thing. No one heard a thing. Nothing was left behind.

We never heard from Ruth again.

Estefani's grandmother, Sofia, who ran the OXXO convenience store down the block from Ruth's salon, had risen earlier than usual to go and open her place. It was December tenth. Sofia was expecting the swarms of pilgrims that would pass by her store, and march down all of Mexico's dirt roads and highways, to get to Mexico City for the Virgin of Guadalupe's day, on December twelfth.

Sofia walked past the beauty salon as she did every day. The door made of corrugated transparent green plastic was swinging wide open into the street. She peered inside and called Ruth's name, but there was no answer.

Later she would explain that she could never tell if those bright red spots on the floor were blood or drops of red nail polish.

Nobody did anything as stupid as calling the police. Instead we waited.

When we walked past the beauty parlor that still had its sign *The Illusion* over the front door, we'd peer in and hope to still see her there. Instead, we only saw two standing hairdryers that our mothers used to sit under and the two empty sinks where Ruth used to wash our hair. The menorah on the windowsill was still there in front of the window that was starred with bullet holes.

We all knew she was stolen.

There are so many dead people out there we're never going to find them alive, my mother said.

José Rosa was so disturbed by the disappearance of Ruth that he spent two months trying to get someone to come from Mexico City to investigate.

There was only one place on that mountain where our cell phones could get a signal from a tower that was twelve kilometers away. This was in a small clearing on the way to school. There was always someone there either talking on their phone or waiting to get a call from a relative in the United States. The clearing was our link to the world. It was here that good news and bad news reached us. My mother named the place Delphi, after a documentary she'd seen on Greek history.

The sounds of the jungle mixed with the noise from the cell phones. The sounds of beeps, rings, songs, and bells that filled the humid air were accompanied by the high-pitch timbre of women's voices.

At this clearing there were always women waiting to hear from their husbands and male children. Some sat there for days that became weeks, months, and years, and their cell phones never rang.

Once my mother was talking to my father, before he left us for good, and I heard her say, I could swallow this telephone I want you so badly.

It was strange to have a man hanging out there. The presence of José Rosa made everyone a little shy. We listened with fascination as he spoke to lawyers, policemen, and judges, and tried to get someone to come and investigate the disappearance of Ruth.

One afternoon, in order to comfort him, Estefani's grandmother, Sofia, placed her hands on his shoulders.

A missing woman is just another leaf that goes down the gutter in a rainstorm, she said.

No one cares about Ruth, my mother added. She was stolen like a car.

The fourth event that defined those twelve months occurred in the last week of the school year, in July. It happened on the day before José Rosa left us to go back to Mexico City.

I was at the schoolroom to help José Rosa clean up and take down the posters he'd placed on the wall during the year. He was getting the room ready for the new teacher who would be arriving in the middle of August.

The poster of the world had been put away. Where I once looked at the shapes of Africa and Australia and stared at the deep blue of the seas and oceans there was now an empty brick wall.

The curtain we'd used to wrap Paula's naked body had never been replaced.

I leaned against the wall that was once covered with a poster of a rainbow and diagrams of light entering and exiting raindrops.

I'm also sad, José Rosa said and walked toward me.

He smelled like black tea with milk and sugar.

He placed his hands on my shoulders and his lips on my lips.

José Rosa tasted like glass windows, cement, and elevators to the moon. His twenty-three-year-old hands held my thirteen-year-old face and he kissed me again. The skyscraper-kiss was mine.

Eight

Run and hide in the hole.

What did you say, Mama?

Run and hide in the hole. Right now. Hush.

What?

Hush. Hush.

My mother had been outside when she saw a tan-colored SUV in the distance. More than actually seeing it, she heard it. There had been a silence in the jungle as the insects and birds grew still.

Quick, she said, run. Run.

I ran out the front door toward the small clearing at the side of the house and under a small palm tree.

The hole was covered with dry palm fronds. I moved the fan-like leaves to one side and scrambled in. From inside, I reached for the fronds and pulled them back over the opening.

The hole was too small. My father had dug it up when I was six years old. I had to lie down on my side with my knees at my chest like skeletal remains of ancient burials I'd seen on television. I could see slivers of light peer in on me through the thatch of leaves.

I heard the sound of a motor approach.

The ground around me trembled as the SUV drove up to our small house and stopped in the clearing, right above the hole and above me.

My small space became dark as I lay in the shadow of the vehicle. Through the leaves I could see the SUV's underbelly, a web of tubes and metal.

Above me the motor was turned off. I could hear the sound of the handbrake as it was cranked into place. The car door opened on the driver's side.

One brown cowboy boot with a high but square and manly heel stepped out of the car.

Those boots did not belong to this land. No one wore boots like that in this heat.

As he stood with the car door open he looked straight at my mother. From the hole I could only see his boots and her red plastic flip-flops face each other.

Good day, Mother, he said.

The man's voice did not belong to this land. The boots and his voice were from the north of Mexico.

Is it always this hot here? he asked. How hot do you think it is?

My mother did not answer.

Ay, Mother, put down that gun.

The other car door opened.

I could not swivel in my hole to try and look around so I just listened.

From the passenger side of the SUV another man stepped out.

Do you want me to shoot her missing? the second man asked. He coughed and wheezed after he spoke. He had an asthmatic voice from the desert, a voice of rattle-snakes and sandstorms.

Where's your daughter, huh? the first man asked.

I don't have a daughter.

Ay, yes you do. Don't lie to me, Mother.

I heard a bullet hit the SUV.

The vehicle shook above me.

I heard the *bratata* explosion of machine gun fire along with the sound of the bullets breaking up the adobe brick walls of our home.

Then it stopped. The jungle swelled and contracted. Insects, reptiles, and birds stilled and nothing rubbed against anything. The sky darkened.

The machine gun had fired the wind out of the mountain.

We were your best hope, Mother, the first man said.

I birthmarked the place, didn't I? I heard the second man say through a shrill wheeze that became a whistle.

The two men got back in the car and slammed the doors shut. The driver turned the key and started the motor. When he placed his boot on the accelerator above me, my hole was filled with the vehicle's exhaust fumes. I opened my mouth and breathed in the noxious smoke.

The car backed up and drove off down the path.

I breathed deeply.

I took in the poison as if it were the smell of a flower or fruit.

My mother made me spend the next two hours in that hole.

You're not coming out until I hear a bird sing, she said.

It was almost dark when she pulled the fronds off of the hole and helped me out. Our little house was sprayed with dozens of bullets. Even the papaya tree had bullet wounds and sweet sap oozed from the holes in the soft bark.

Just look at that, my mother said.

I turned. She was pointing at the hole with her finger.

I peered in and saw four albino-shell scorpions there. The deadliest kind.

Those scorpions showed you more mercy than any human being ever will, my mother said.

She took off one of her flip-flops and killed all four in beating blows.

Mercy is not a two-way street, she said. Then she scooped them up in her hand and threw them to one side.

When we lifted up the fronds in order to cover the hole again, we found a blue plastic asthma inhaler. It was on the ground where the second man had fired his weapon at my house and trees.

What do we do with it? I asked. I was afraid to touch it.

I bet he doesn't come back for it, my mother said.

But that man won't be able to breathe.

Just leave it there. Don't touch it.

The next day, up the mountain at the clearing where the cell phones sometimes worked, we found out that those men had succeeded in stealing Paula.

Maria was sitting off alone under a tree pinching her harelip scar. Estefani's mother, Augusta, was standing straight in the middle of the clearing with her cellular phone held high above her head as she tried to get a signal. Estefani's grandmother, Sofia, was talking frantically to someone.

Paula's mother, Concha, sat and stared at her phone as if her eyes could will it to ring. Call me, call me, Paula, call me, she whispered into the phone.

My mother sat down next to Concha.

They came to our house first, my mother said.

Concha lifted up her face and looked at me. Did you get into your hole? she asked.

Yes. I was in the hole.

Paula didn't make it. The dogs didn't bark. We didn't hear them coming. The dogs didn't bark.

Concha had the meanest, scariest dogs anyone had ever seen. They were injured animals run over by cars that she picked up off the highway. She had at least ten dogs soaking up the shade in the trees around her house. Mostly they were ugly inbreeds. My mother used to say that those dogs needed poison.

Concha held the cellular phone high above her head.

I never heard them kill the dogs, Concha said.

They killed the dogs?

Paula and I were watching television, Concha said. We'd just finished bathing and we were wrapped in our towels, cooling off, sitting on the couch. I heard a noise behind me. He could have touched us. I didn't hear him. He pointed a pistol at me. He used his other hand to curl his finger at Paula. You're coming with me, he said but he didn't really say it. His finger said it as it curled again and again. Paula stood, holding the towel around her body. She walked over to the man and they both walked out the door and into the SUV. She was still in her towel, only her towel.

Concha followed them outside and watched the SUV disappear down the road. The area around the house was covered with the bleeding bodies of her dead dogs. The television was still playing loudly inside.

Barefoot, wrapped in a towel, Concha said again and shook her head.

Under the lemon tree, at the edge of her small plot of land, was the hole she'd dug years ago for Paula to hide in.

I buried the dogs in there, Concha said. I just buried them one on top of the other in Paula's hole.

That day Mike was up on the clearing. He chewed his gum rhythmically with only his front teeth. The white lump would appear and disappear behind his lips. I had not seen him for a few weeks since he spent most of his time in Acapulco. He always stood apart from everyone else with his arm held high, telephone in the air, searching for a signal. He had at least five phones spread out around his body, in all his pockets. He sounded like a music box of ringtones, vibrations, bells, and rap and electronic music. He said he had a US telephone, Mexico City telephone, Florida telephone, and several Acapulco telephones. It was Maria who told me he was selling marijuana. This was the reason he had money. We didn't care. Thanks to Mike it was Christmas on our mountain every month of the year. He was always buying presents for everyone.

If Mike was home, he spent his time up at the clearing. He'd receive calls from all over the USA and Europe. He even had a Facebook page and Twitter account. It seemed that everyone in the USA knew that Mike was the guy to buy drugs from in Mexico. Maria said that Mike was famous in the United States. During US holidays, tourists, especially kids on Spring Break, ordered their drugs from him before arriving in Acapulco. His nickname was Mister Wave.

Mike was plugged into his iPod all day so it was impossible to talk to him. He listened to hip-hop and rap and was constantly skipping and moving to a beat. He even spoke with a beat to his words. If he'd had a dream, it would have been to be a hip-hop dancer in New York City. If he'd had a dream, but he didn't. His life moved from weekend to weekend as if those seven days, from Monday to Sunday, were a season.

On the day Paula was stolen he switched his iPod to off and burrowed it deep in the front pocket of his jeans.

That day all anyone could hear was the silence of cell phones. That was it. It was the sound of Paula stolen. That was the song.

Nine

The next day was the first day without Paula.

The new teacher had a completely different approach to his job. Mr Rosa had been diligent and had followed the Secretariat of Public Education's curriculum. Our new teacher, Rafael de la Cruz, didn't care. All he wanted to do was to get his year of social service over and done with and go back to Guadalajara, his hometown, where his fiancée lived. Instead of having lessons, we'd sit in class and listen to music. He brought a CD player and two portable speakers to our classroom. We had never listened to classical music before.

Every morning we'd get to school and sit down in our chairs and wait for Mr de la Cruz to arrive. He was always late. When he'd finally arrive, sometimes up to two hours late, he'd walk into the room, take the CD player and the speakers out of a small suitcase, and say, So you're all still here. I was never sure what that was supposed to mean. Where would we be?

He only played Tchaikovsky. *Swan Lake* floated out of our schoolroom, across our jungle, over our homes, hills covered in poppies and marijuana plants, down the black oily highway, and across the Sierra Madre, until the sound of swans dancing covered the whole country.

He must be a homosexual! my mother said.

The new teacher had no interest in us. I liked him. He came to the school, played music, and went back to his little one-room house and never came out of that room until the next day. But, in that schoolroom, for four or five hours, he made us cross our arms on our white plastic desks and lay our heads down, close our eyes, and listen.

During these concerts, Estefani would fall asleep and later complain that the music actually made her feel cold. After she figured out this was all we were going to do for the year, she brought a blanket to school and covered her back and shoulders. As Estefani's mother, Augusta, became sicker from AIDS, Estefani became colder. The mother was sucking the heat out of the daughter.

Maria, who was the best cumbia and salsa dancer around, didn't mind listening to this music. As long as she didn't have to do mathematics, she was happy.

On those mornings I laid my head on my arms and closed my eyes. Within Tchaikovsky's music, I heard the earth quake below the ground. I heard tree roots spread under the land. I heard poppies open their petals.

I listened for Paula's voice, but I heard nothing.

I was sure she was dead. We were all sure she was dead. So, when she came back, my mother said, Oh my, the coffin has been opened and she walked out of it.

That was the last year that we went to school. A Primary School diploma was a door out of childhood. The truth is some of us were twelve, thirteen or even fourteen when this happened because it took forever to graduate. There were years when teachers simply gave up and left halfway through or years no teacher ever even showed up.

The only reason we graduated was that Mr de la Cruz didn't care if we knew anything or not. He announced that there would be no final exams and he signed the diplomas and got out of there as fast as he could. I was sure he thought it was a great success to have left our part of the world without a bullet hole in his body.

Now that school was over we had to think about what we were going to do. Estefani knew she had no choice. She was going to spend these next years watching her mother die. Maria was going to wait and see. Mike was bringing more money home and was pushing for Maria and his mother to leave this mountain and move to Acapulco. He said he was going to buy them a house. Nobody even asked what Paula would do as she now lived like a baby and was locked up in her house all day.

My mother said to me, You're not going to sell iguanas on the side of the road. You're not going to go to the beauty parlor school in Acapulco. You're not going to be a maid in Mexico City. You're not going to work in a factory on the border. You're not going to stay here doing nothing and you better not get pregnant or I'll kill you.

One day my mother and I were up on the clearing when Mike came over and stood next to us. He literally seemed to hop to the music of the cell phones in all his pockets that rang and chimed and jangled and buzzed. He fidgeted and wriggled inside of himself as if his bones were strutting inside the clothing of skin. As a young boy he used to walk around with a pet iguana tied to a string. He was heartbroken when his mother stewed that iguana in a pot with carrots and potatoes.

From one of his pockets Mike pulled out a gold chain

and gave it to my mother. I've always wanted to give you something pretty, Rita, he said. You've got enough ugly in your house.

Mike said he knew of a family in Acapulco who needed help with their small child and was looking for a nanny.

That's perfect, my mother said. That's perfect for you, Ladydi.

You'll have to live in Acapulco most of the week, Mike explained. You'll make pretty money. These people are rich, rich, rich. Mike punctuated the word rich by snapping his fingers three times: snap, snap, snap.

My mother stood up straight when she heard the family was rich. I knew she was thinking of all the things I could steal and bring home. In the mirror of her eyes, I was filling up my bag with a lipstick and a bottle of shampoo.

I knew what it would mean to leave. I knew my mother would fall asleep with her jaw dropped and her mouth agape. The television would be tuned to the History Channel and words about castles in France or the history of chess would fill the room. She would be surrounded by empty beer bottles. Long black ants would crawl in and out of her mouth and there would not be a daughter around to flick them away.

Yes, I said to Mike. Yes.

As my mother and I left the clearing and walked back home together we moved past the tree where we'd buried the corpse years ago before Paula was stolen. We never found out whom that young man belonged to. No one ever came around asking. The jungle has ears all over, my mother said. There are no secrets here.

That afternoon I found out what had happened to Paula.

I was walking down the path that led to the schoolroom, when I ran into Paula sitting under a tree. She was sitting on the ground, which we never did. On our mountain we always placed something between our skin and the earth.

She was wearing a long dress that covered her like a tent. I knew that insects were crawling up her bare legs under the cloth.

I felt the warm, black earth under my feet.

The ground had brought us together.

I wanted to hold her hand. Her face was bent over as she looked at something in her lap.

I walked slowly toward her, the way I had learned to walk when I wanted to catch a small garter snake or a baby iguana. As I approached, my body came between her body and the sun and I covered her with the eclipse of my shadow.

She looked up and I sat next to her on the ground. I knew I'd be brushing black and red ants off my skin within a minute. Paula's dress was covered with black ants swarming all over. A few had already migrated up her clothes, crawled around her neck and behind her ears. She did not flick them off.

Don't you feel so sorry for Britney Spears? Paula said.

The long sleeves of Paula's dress were folded over and pushed up. On her left arm, the inside where the skin is pale and thin like guava skin, I could see a row of cigarette burns, circles, polka dots, pink circles.

You know, Paula continued, Britney has many tattoos.

Yes? No, I didn't know.

Oh yes. She has a fairy and small daisy circling her toe.

No, I didn't know.

And she has a butterfly and another flower and a small star on her right hand.

Oh. Really?

Yes. Her body is like a garden.

Do you know who I am? I asked.

Oh yes, of course. You're Ladydi.

I brushed a few ants off her legs and arms. Get up, I said. The ants are going to eat you alive if you sit here any longer.

The ants?

Does your mother know where you are?

I took hold of her wrists and helped lift her up. I will take you home, I said.

Let me be with you for a little longer. I like you, Paula said. You're nice to me.

I held her hand and walked with her toward a log a few steps away.

We can't sit on the ground, I said.

We sat down, side by side, looking forward as if we were on a bus heading down a highway. I took her hand in mine and looked at the pattern of cigarette burns on the inside belly-skin of her arm.

I've seen tigers and lions, she said. Real ones. It wasn't a zoo.

Tell me.

At that place there was a garage for the cars and a garage for the animals.

You can tell me.

Paula described the ranch. It was in the north of Mexico, in the state of Tamaulipas, right on the US border. An important drug trafficker, who was known by the nickname McClane after Bruce Willis's character in the movie *Die Hard*, lived with his wife and four children. McClane had been a policeman.

I was his slave-mistress, Paula said.

Slave-mistress?

Yes. We call ourselves that. All of us do.

At one end of the ranch there was a garage that housed McClane's cars, which included four BMWs, two Jaguars, and several pickup trucks and SUVs. Next to the garage there were cement rooms that contained a lion and three tigers. Paula learned from the caretakers that the animals had been bought from zoos in the United States. The property also contained its own small cemetery with four large mausoleums that were the size of little houses. Each mausoleum even had a bathroom.

It wasn't a zoo. Every day the lion and tiger excrement was picked up and wrapped into drug shipments bound for the United States. This practice kept the drug-sniffing border dogs away from the shipments.

Paula's job on the ranch was to sleep with McClane every now and again and to help pack the lion and tiger excrement around the drugs or rub a small film of the excrement on the outside of plastic packages.

Someone told me they were fed human meat, Paula said.

The sky began to darken as we sat on the log holding hands. In the dusk, small clouds of mosquitoes began to surround us, but since Paula continued to talk I sat there and let them bite. She didn't seem to notice the feeling of insects crawling on or biting her skin.

I don't need to tell you that along the way I was a plastic water bottle, right? Paula said. I was something you pick up and take a swig of.

I shook my head. No, no.

Those guys who stole me were from Matamoros. They took me north to that party. It was McClane's daughter's birthday party. She was fifteen.

A whole circus had been rented for the party. Several

large tents had been set up in a field to one side of the ranch house. A man walked around giving away clouds of pink cotton candy on long wood sticks. There was a band and a large dance floor.

Paula was taken to one of the tents that had been placed very far away from the party. She could hardly hear the band play. Inside this tent there were a few men and over thirty women. Rows of plastic chairs were set up at one side of the tent. In the middle of the open space there was a table with Cokes, beers, plastic glasses, and paper plates piled high with peanuts covered in red chili powder. The women in the tent had been stolen. The drug traffickers, who'd killed Paula's mother's dogs and had stolen her wrapped naked in a white towel, were now going to sell her.

McClane was in the tent. He looked at the women and asked them to smile. He wanted to see their teeth. But he didn't look into Paula's mouth.

McClane picked Paula. He picked the most beautiful girl in Mexico. She should have been a legend. Her face should have covered magazines. Love songs should have been written to her.

On the log beside me, Paula continued to look straight ahead as she spoke. When she seemed to grow tired she continued to tell her story only as a mix of impressions.

You don't need to know about the sun rising and setting, she said. You don't need to know what I ate or where I slept. You need to know that McClane had over two hundred pairs of boots. They were made from every kind of animal and reptile that was in Noah's Ark. He had a pair made from donkey penises. One pair he liked to wear on Sundays. These were a pale yellow and everyone said they were made of human flesh.

Paula's impressions tumbled out of her as if they were a list she'd penciled down on a paper. She said that McClane's daughter had over two hundred Barbie dolls. One doll had been dipped in gold and had real green emeralds for eyes. McClane had a box filled with feathers from the cocks he raised for cock fights. McClane had a scar across his belly as if he'd almost been cut in half by a magician. The sons all had their own toy cars. These were real cars, but miniatures, that even ran on gasoline. The ranch had a miniature gas station and a miniature OXXO store beside it.

The women that Paula met in the tent, and saw at other times at parties, were Gloria, Aurora, Isabel, Esperanza, Lupe, Lola, Claudia, and Mercedes.

Who are those women? I asked.

Oh, girls like me, she said. And the daughter had a small house to play in with toilets that flushed.

How much did you cost?

Oh, I was a present.

Why do you have those cigarette burns on your arm?

Oh, but we all have them, Ladydi. She looked down at the inside of her arm, stretching it out before her as if she were showing me the page of a book.

If you've been stolen, you burn the inside of your left arm with cigarettes.

Why? I don't understand.

Are you crazy? she asked. Are you stupid?

I'm sorry.

A woman decided it a long, long time ago and now we all do it, she said. If we're found dead someplace everyone will know we were stolen. It is our mark. My cigarette burns are a message.

I looked at the pattern of circles on her arm as she

continued to hold her limb, stretched out like an oar into the jungle air.

You do want people to know it's you. Otherwise how will our mothers find us?

It was almost dark.

We have to go now, I said. Come with me. I'll take you.

Her mother was standing at the front door waiting. She held a baby bottle filled with milk in one hand.

It's time for my baby to go to bed, Concha said. What on earth were you doing out in the jungle?

Paula didn't answer and went straight into the house.

Her mother walked me out to the edge of their property.

Did she say anything to you? Concha asked. Don't say anything to anyone, Concha said in a panic. How did they know she was here? Who watched and knew a beautiful girl lived up here? They came for her. They knew what they were coming for. If they know she's back, if they find out, they'll come back and get her. We have to leave. There's no time. In a day or so. I've been planning. Ladydi, we're escaping. What did she tell you?

She told me about the cigarette burns.

Did she tell you that she did it to herself? Did she tell you that all the women who have been robbed do this to themselves?

I nodded.

Do you believe her? Concha asked. I don't believe it at all. I can't even imagine burning myself. That's impossible.

Yes. I believe it.

At that moment Paula appeared behind her mother. She was like a white vaporous creature. She held a baby bottle in one hand. She was naked. In the dark, under a river of moonlight, I could see the nipples of her breasts, the black hair between her legs and the constellation of cigarette burns all over her body. I could see the cigarette-burn stars that made up Orion and Taurus. Even her feet were covered in the round burns. Paula had walked through the Milky Way and every star had burned her body.

Ten

Concha turned and picked up Paula in her arms as if she were a four-year-old girl and carried her into their house. That was the last time I ever saw Concha and Paula.

We knew they were gone when Concha's three dogs appeared near our house rummaging for food. They were stray dogs Concha had picked up after her other dogs had been slaughtered the day Paula was stolen.

Why didn't she kill those damn dogs before she left? my mother said. We're not taking care of them. Don't give them anything to eat Ladydi, do you hear?

We went over to Paula's house to see if they'd left or not.

As we reached the small two-room house everything looked as if Paula and her mother were about to return.

Yes, my mother said. This is how you disappear: as if you're going to appear.

There was a fresh and full carton of milk on the small kitchen table and the television was turned on. The sound of the news from Acapulco filled the room: there'd been a shootout at a bar. Two new morgues were being built. A severed head had been found on the beach.

My mother started to poke around that house and it was that kind of poking around that I knew too well. She picked up a half-full bottle of tequila, an electric coffee maker and a large bag of potato chips.

You go and look in Paula's room and see what she's left behind. Maybe there're some jeans or T-shirts you can use, she said.

Her small bed was there. It was raised up from the ground on a pile of bricks. This kept her away from the mouse-sized cockroaches that crawled around the floor at night. The wall was covered with dozens of huge, thick nails on which she'd hung her clothes so that her wall looked like a collage of cloth. I could see several pairs of plastic flip-flops and a pair of tennis shoes lined up in a row under her bed. There were two empty baby bottles lying on the pillow and a shoebox on her bed.

I opened the shoebox.

The jungle heat filled my mouth. Ants and spiders were running through my blood.

There were a few photographs in the shoebox. I looked deep into the small black eyes of the man who had squeezed the sweet girl out of Paula's body. The photos were of a man and his family. The man was dressed in a red-and-white-checkered shirt, jeans with a wide leather belt that had an oval silver buckle. He was also wearing black, high-heeled cowboy boots. These people were from the north of Mexico. Their clothes told that story. It was McClane.

I took the photographs out of the box and stuffed them down into my jeans. At the bottom of the box there was a small notebook, which I placed into my back pocket.

My mother appeared in the doorway.

It's horrible to think, but someone must have been watching Paula for years, my mother said. They were just watching her grow up.

She was holding the bottle of tequila in one hand and the bag of potato chips in the other.

She'd been picked out a long time ago, my mother said. She'd been watched the way we watch an apple on a tree: we watch it grow until it's ripe and then we pick it.

As we walked home, I could feel the dry, thin cardboard photographs tucked down the front of my jeans as I moved. My mother had left her flat, white plastic sandals behind and was wearing Concha's bright green plastic flip-flops that had a red plastic flower attached to the front straps. My mother followed my eyes and looked down at her feet.

Well, Ladydi, she said, Concha's not going to use them anymore, right?

My mother was carrying the bottle of tequila and the bags of chips.

We walked in silence for a while and then my mother suddenly turned her head and spat on the ground.

If anyone wants to create a symbol or a flag for our piece of earth on Earth it should be a plastic flip-flop, she said.

When we got home the front door was open and Mike was sitting inside our house waiting for us. It seemed strange to me that he would wait inside. People did not do that. They did not go inside a house and sit down when there was no one home. Our house even smelled strongly of his cologne, which had a minty smell, like chewing gum.

He sat in the kitchen with the refrigerator door wide open the way people sit in front of a fire. Two telephones rested on his thigh. I could see that Mike had begun to grow out his hair, which he had shaved off a few years ago, so that it looked like small bushy tufts of black grass all over his head.

So, you were confused and thought this was your house? my mother said to Mike.

She placed the tequila and chips on the kitchen table.

Shut that door! she commanded.

Now don't get angry, Little Mother, he said, standing up quickly and closing the refrigerator door with one swipe of his hand.

Mike called all the older women on our hill *Little Mother*. Even my mother, who didn't take sweetness from anyone, seemed to like it. I knew she was about to scream at him for coming into our house, snooping around and opening up the fridge, but the words *Little Mother* stopped her. It was as if the words caressed her and could make her purr.

On our mountain a refrigerator was our most important appliance, piece of furniture, or whatever one wanted to call it. It was our door to the North Pole, polar bears, seals, and glaciers. On a hot day everyone sat around it with the door wide open. During the day we kept our pillows inside to cool them. The cotton pillows rested among cans of beer, a box of eggs and packets of cheese wrapped in plastic. At night, for an hour or so, our heads would rest on cool cotton. When one side of the pillow warmed up, we'd just flip it over. The pillow cooled down our minds and dreams. My mother was the inventor of this idea. Everyone on the mountain did it.

The refrigerator was one of the main things my mother prayed to. She said that a cold beer could make you love a refrigerator.

My mother poured herself a small shot of tequila and opened the bag of chips with her teeth.

So, what's up? she asked Mike.

Mike explained that he would meet me down on the highway on Monday morning, which was in two days, and that we'd take the bus together to Acapulco. I had an appointment to meet the family I was going to work with at eleven in the morning. I should pack a bag and be ready to stay there.

I left my mother drinking in our little house and walked Mike some of the way down to the highway. I wanted to ask him about Maria. Now that we no longer went to school, I rarely saw Maria. I didn't like to go to Maria's house because it was hard to face the fact that her mother, Luz, had been my father's mistress. Everyone on the mountain knew the scandal and Mike knew, of course, as he knew everything about everyone. The only person who did not know who she was, was Maria. The only person who did not know that her harelip had been God's curse was Maria. I wanted to tell her she was my half-sister and wanted her to love me even more as her sister, but I was so afraid that she would hate me if she knew who she really was.

I told Mike to tell Maria that I wanted to see her. I asked him to tell her to meet me at the schoolroom late that afternoon.

Mike skipped down the mountain to a tune of three cell phones all suddenly ringing at the same time. It was as if the reception dead zone had opened in the air and a phone signal came down on him like lightning.

When I turned to walk back to my house, I remembered the photographs that were still stuffed down the front of my pants. I reached in and took out the square photos printed on soft cardboard.

There were six photographs. One was of a man, who I assumed to be McClane standing on an airstrip next to a small plane. Two other photographs were of women standing against a wall in groups. Paula was in both of these. Another photograph was of McClane standing in front of a row of medieval suits of armor. It looked as if he was inside a castle.

The last two photographs in the group were of a large red horse trailer. It was a small unit capable of holding two or three horses, the kind that can be pulled by a pickup truck or an SUV. One of the photographs had been taken with care to show the blood spilling out of the door.

When I got back home, my mother was in a frenzy killing flies with a flyswatter. The weather had been so hot over the past month there was an epidemic of flies. These were the fat, juicy kind of flies, with spiky fur on their backs. When this fly bites it leaves a big red welt that hurts for days. There were black, bloody specks all over our kitchen table and floor.

Get down on your knees and pray for the flyswatter, my mother said. Who left the goddamned door open?

You know, I said.

My mother gave me a look, a nasty look, and continued to swat at the flies. I recognized the flyswatter she'd stolen from the Reyes' house at least two years ago. Pray for the flyswatter, she said.

My mother hated those flies but she loved to kill them. It was a happy bloodbath in that small kitchen.

She knew, what we all knew, the flies always win.

I ran past my mother and the dead black and red flies, and hid Paula's photographs in my room under my mattress.

When I walked back out to the kitchen, my mother was sitting at the table with the flyswatter lying across her lap. Bloody pieces of squashed flies were embedded in the plastic netting. She was taking a deep swig, almost half the bottle of beer, in one great swallow. Then she pulled the bottle from her lips. It made a hollow sucking sound.

I sat down in the middle of the massacre.

I am so angry, my mother said.

What happened?

On the television they were talking about a magazine that is publishing an issue about what it is to be a woman!

So?

I'd tell them the truth.

What's the truth, Mama?

A woman's world is in her panties.

Yes?

Do you think those Mexico City women writers are going to write about the sadness? Yes, the sadness when you find there is blood there and this means one thing. You're beginning to lose your baby!

What are you saying, Mama? I asked.

Between the fly massacre and the rant about panties, I was worried about her. The look in her eyes reminded me of the look she'd had on her face when our mountain was hit by a bad earthquake. Later, after the earthquake, after it was all over, she said we should have known.

Two weeks before the earthquake our little two-room house had been invaded by every creature around. Black widows, red tarantulas, and white transparent and brown scorpions began to show up everywhere. Red ants were crawling all over the ceiling. We found a nest of snakes, like a knot of black ribbons, behind the television.

My mother's reaction to this was to watch the television all day and all night. She didn't cook and I had to rummage around for a dry tortilla and cheese and even open up a can of tuna fish, which we would normally never eat because she decided one day that it tasted like cat food. My mother watched television because it was the only way out of our mountain.

As I killed as many insects as I could and ate dried mango strips, she traveled to Petra and visited a family of Bedouins who had been expelled from their cave and were now living in Bedouin Village, which was cement government housing. Their camel lived in their cement garage. My mother traveled to India where she watched medical tourists have cheap operations. She watched the Miss Universe contest. On the History Channel she sat through six episodes on Henry VIII's wives.

During one of those pre-earthquake days a stray sheep appeared at our doorway. I had gone outside to get away from the television and my mother and there it was, sitting on the ground in the shade of a papaya tree.

When I went inside to tell my mother about it, she just looked through me and said, Next thing you'll tell me is that Mary and Joseph are outside and need a place to sleep.

These were the first words she'd said in days. But then she turned away from me and looked back at the program on the objects that have been found in the bellies of dead sharks. A man was cutting open the shark's belly on the deck of a ship and pulling out a wedding ring.

I went outside and gave the sheep some water. The animal lapped it up with its small tongue. It was the first time I'd seen blue eyes in real life and not on television.

When I went back inside the house, the sheep followed me in.

My mother turned and looked at it and said, That is not a sheep, Ladydi, that's a lamb, just in time for the slaughter.

I was not exactly sure what she meant by that. It could mean that we were going to kill the lamb and eat it for supper or maybe she was into biblical sayings now that we had become the Noah's Ark for insects.

Since I had looked into the animal's blue eyes, I knew I could not eat it. I ended up shooing it out of our house and down the mountain. I hoped a large silver passenger bus on the way to Acapulco did not run it over it.

The reason for all that craziness on the mountain was the earthquake. On the news, we heard that the epicenter had been just outside the port of Acapulco.

That's us, my mother said with excitement. We live outside the port of Acapulco! Of course it was right here, under us!

That earthquake hit at seven thirty that morning. We were having breakfast when our two-room house began to shake. Outside we watched the ground move in waves as if it were made of water.

On the day my mother killed the flies, ranted about praying to panties, and was drinking too much, I felt scared. She was breaking. I could see the shards.

What are you trying to tell me, Mama? I said. Be clear.

My mother threw her head back and rolled her eyes.

Yes, yes, yes. Some days I pulled, tore with my teeth, the skin around the sides of my fingernails and gave them to you to eat.

Are you saying this?

You were not even a year old. I mixed it in the rice. What did you want me to do? There are women who have cut off slabs of skin from their bodies to feed their children. I heard about that on TV.

Shit, Mama, I said.

What's the difference between that and mother's milk? You tell me?

No, Mother, I said. Those fancy Mexico City writers are not going to write about that!

God only knew if any of this was true. My mother placed

lying in the category of stealing. Why should one tell the truth about something, if you can lie instead? This was her philosophy. If my mother took the bus, she said she took a taxi.

It was going to be a long afternoon until she passed out. The tequila bottle from Paula's house was empty. My mother stood and took another beer from the fridge.

I killed them, she said, so you can clean them up.

I grabbed an old rag by the sink and started to wipe the dead flies off the chairs, tabletops and walls.

A few hours later when I left to meet Maria at the schoolroom, my mother was on her fifth beer. She was lying on her bed fanning herself with a piece of cardboard she'd ripped off the side of a cornflakes cereal box. The television was on full blast. In her stupor, she was watching a program about wild animals in the Amazon.

Why doesn't NatGeo come here and film our mountain? Mother asked.

As I walked away from my house, I stopped and looked back. Our small two-room structure had long rusty girders sticking out toward a second floor that was never built. All the houses on the mountain were like this. We built with the dream of a second floor. But, instead of second floors, we all had parabolic antennas. If our mountain were seen from space, it would look like a white land made of thousands of opened umbrellas.

Maria was at the schoolroom. She was sitting at her old desk and looked like a portrait of our childhood. Her hair was fixed up in a round bun at the top of her head. We called this her onion hairdo. It was pulled so tight she could not blink properly.

Every time I looked at her, and saw my father in her face, I had to stop myself from telling her the truth.

Sometimes I even thought that the only reason I could remember what my father looked like was because Maria was there to remind me. When my mother found out that my father had another family over there she burned all his photographs on the stove, just like tortillas. One after the other they curled and toasted on the stovetop until they turned into black, gray ash. I watched his Sinatra smile and my birthday cakes and birthday balloons float out the door in smoke.

The scar from Maria's harelip had faded. But when I looked at her I always saw the old face, the vulnerable old face that was mythical and painful. The scar had gone, but that harelip still made her who she was.

I sat down at my old school desk right next to hers. We had sat like this for years. Our dry, scratchy, little-girl elbows used to touch as we practiced our penmanship and numbers. In this room we had been able to leave our homes and the jungle and dream about a different kind of life.

Maria told me that Augusta, Estefani's mother, was running a high fever and that they were leaving tomorrow morning for Mexico City where there was an AIDS charity that gave her the pills she needed. Augusta had been sick with AIDS now for over six years and these trips back and forth to the city had become routine.

I told Maria that Paula and Concha had left the mountain forever.

I told Maria about the photographs. When Maria heard about the photographs she stood up.

Ruth? Maria said. Did you ask about Ruth?

On the mountain everyone was sure that the disappearance of Ruth and the stealing of Paula were related.

I shook my head.

I didn't ask. I'm sorry, I said.

I watched Maria rub her finger over her harelip scar. The day of the operation I watched my mother and Ruth smoke a whole pack of Salem cigarettes. The menthol smoke filled the beauty parlor. As little girls Maria and I used to steal the butts from Ruth's ashtray and suck on the filters as if they were a Halls mentho-lyptus. I could taste the mint filters as I looked at Maria's face.

Did you look at them carefully? Did you look and see if one of the women in the photos was Ruth?

No.

Let's go.

We stood and marched out of the schoolroom toward my house. We walked quickly, almost skipping, filled with the hope of finding Ruth's face in the photographs. In our foolish dream we ran through the jungle filled with a silly joy.

It was that fast, fast like an arm that becomes a snake. Her arm moved. I saw the shadow on the wall and then, so fast, like when a scorpion lifts up its tail or an iguana zaps its tongue out into a hive-like vapor of gnats. That fast. My mother had the small silver pistol in her hand and everything was ready. It was as if the whole Sierra Madre grew still. I heard the sound of crushed bone and that was a sound I'd never heard before.

I heard the sound of crushed bone as that bullet went into Maria, into my half-sister, into my father's other daughter, into the daughter that looked just like him.

This can happen after ten bottles of beer mixed with tequila. If they'd drawn my mother's blood into a syringe, her blood would have been yellow. If her blood had been placed in a test tube and held up to the light it would have been pure Corona. But no one would do a test or call the police on our mountain.

Calling the police was like inviting a scorpion into your house. Who does that? my mother always said.

What happened to my mother that afternoon? The light held that moment between afternoon and dusk. In that light, that is almost not light, who did she think was at her threshold?

I knelt beside Maria and looked into my father's face. I looked at her face and it was like looking into a lake. Under the surface, as if I could see a lakebed of stones and silver fish, I could see her torn face, the stitches, and the scars of the harelip.

I could feel the warm blood in my hands as I opened her clothes to look at the wound.

When Maria opened her eyes we looked at each other.

What was that? she asked.

Where the hell did you get that gun, Mother? I spat the words at my mother as I placed my hand around Maria's waist.

Mike.

I wanted to hold on to my mother as she faded and left the planet forever just as Maria's blood baptized our piece of jungle.

Take me back to a minute ago; take me back to a minute ago, my mother said.

The clocks were turning backward in her mind. Rewind, she was thinking. Press rewind.

My mother had always told me that death was on time and never late.

The room darkened from a cloud moving overhead. I could hear the sound of a parrot outside.

As my mother sat down in a heap on the floor she said, She'll be fine. It was just a scratch.

I wrapped Maria's arm in a dishtowel and placed my

arm around her waist. Together we stumbled out of the house and down our mountain.

There was no one on the highway. A few large passenger buses whizzed by. The black asphalt burned under our plastic flip-flops and the heat made the car oil on the road turn blue and green.

After standing in that devil heat for twenty minutes a few taxis drove past but it seemed to take forever to get a taxi to stop and take us to the hospital. No taxi drivers want blood in their cars. As soon as I said we were going to the hospital, they took one look at Maria's face. When their eyes followed her face down to her arm, which was wrapped in a dishtowel, the taxi drivers hit the accelerator and took off. In Guerrero there are some taxis that have a cardboard sign on their dashboard that says *No Bloody Bodies.*

I kept looking at Maria's arm and hoping the dishrag could contain or even stop the flow.

A taxi driver finally stopped and agreed to take us.

He looked at Maria's arm.

No, I'm not bringing that in here unless you put it in a plastic bag, he said.

He reached over to the glove compartment, took out a plastic supermarket bag, and handed it to me.

Put the arm inside it.

What did he say? Maria asked.

Put your arm in the bag or you're not getting in here.

I carefully took Maria's wounded arm and placed it in the supermarket bag as if it were a leg of lamb.

Okay, her arm is in the bag, I said. Let's go!

Knot it at the end.

Sorry?

Tie it up.

I took the ends of the bag and made a small knot with the corners of the plastic at the top of her arm. She let me do this to her without protest. It was as if, now that my mother had shot it, her arm belonged to my family.

So, who were you bothering? the taxi driver asked as we drove down the highway.

The only people in all of Mexico who knew what was going on in the country were the taxi drivers. If we wanted to know about something that had happened, we'd say, Take a taxi. It seemed to me that someone should get all the taxi drivers together, someone like Jacobo Zabludovsky (the old journalist who my mother swore was the very last noble person in the whole of Mexico), and ask them what the hell was going on in our country. My mother always said that there is a taxi driver out there who knew exactly what had happened to Paula and Ruth.

The drive to Acapulco took less than an hour. I wanted to tell Maria that she was my half-sister and that my mother had shot her because, in my mother's drunken state, she thought that Maria was our father. But I had to keep quiet because I knew that taxi driver's ears were standing on end to hear the news.

The man had a boxer's hands: huge knuckles covered in scars. He gripped the steering wheel fiercely. The man even turned off his radio in order to hear any information that might come out of the back seat.

So, who were you bothering? the taxi driver asked again.

I decided not to answer and held Maria in the circle of my arm.

He looked at us in his rearview mirror.

You must have been a bad, bad girl to deserve a shooting, right?

He was a man with black curly hair shot with gray. He had deep smile wrinkles at the edges of his eyes.

It was an accident, I said.

An accident? That's what everyone says.

Please.

She's a bad girl, he said as if Maria were not there. He's going to go to jail; you know that, don't you?

Yes.

He's going to go to jail. As soon as they see a gunshot wound in the emergency room the doctors there, you know, well, they have to notify the police. That's a law.

It was an accident.

I bet it hurts.

I pressed my lips together. His face never stopped looking at mine in the rearview mirror. I had to keep looking away. He was observing me more than watching the road.

That must really hurt, he said.

It sure does, I answered.

Hey, doesn't your friend know how to talk? I've always said if someone doesn't talk then they're hiding a thing or something.

Yes, it hurts, I said. She can't talk because it hurts.

Why don't you let me see your little boobies? he said. I'll give you your money back if you show me. Your hurt friend doesn't have to show me anything, just you.

Maybe another day, I said.

You remind me of my daughter. You're a marzipan.

I looked over at Maria who was pale. She mouthed the word *asshole.*

I squirmed forward in my seat. Then I reached around my back and lifted up my skirt. I peed deep through my underwear and into the black cloth seat of the taxi. I felt the wet heat from my urine surround my bare thighs. My mother had taught me about revenge. I knew this would have made her proud of me.

I turned and held Maria's arm and tried to stroke her head a little, which was hard because of Maria's stiff, onion-bun hairdo. I looked at her arm in the plastic supermarket bag but it was not filling up. Maria gave me an intense look and tilted her head toward the side of her body. The blood was not going into the plastic bag. As she was holding her arm, it was being pulled backward and down, through the tie in the plastic supermarket bag, down the side of her body. I could see that the red, short-sleeved blouse above her ribs was drenched.

At this point Maria's head lolled backward and her eyes closed.

I thought she had died.

Maria, wake up, wake up, I whispered.

The taxi driver turned around and looked at us. Missy, she better die so I can leave you both at the side of the road.

She's not dead.

If she dies, I'm leaving you both at the side of the road. I hope she dies because I want to get rid of both of you.

When I saw the enormous gray bay surrounded by a wall of hotels and condominiums and smelled the salt, I knew Maria was going to live. She was curled against me, under my arm. I kissed the top of her head, which smelled like greasy coconut hair oil, with love because she was my sister and she was going to know about this very soon. While I still had the secret, I could love her.

When I saw the bay I remembered coming to Acapulco for the first time. My father was still living with us and we'd come to visit him at work. He was a bartender at a small hotel at that time. I remember my mother got dressed up in a white dress that had a halter top so that her back was exposed. She wore high white heels and bright red lipstick. She also dressed me up in a red sundress and combed my hair into two braids.

We're going to surprise your father and we have to look pretty, like girls, for the surprise, my mother said.

She carried her heels in one hand and walked in her flip-flops down to the highway to catch the bus.

On the bus ride she checked her lipstick in a small mirror that she carried in her purse. He arms were still slightly red in places, as she'd spent the whole morning plucking the black hair out of her forearms with tweezers.

From the bus station we took a taxi to the hotel where my father worked.

The hotel faced the bay. My father worked at the bar that was outside, beside the swimming pool and under a large thatched roof of palm fronds. The sunlight broke through small spaces in the roofing and made the glass of the liquor bottles shine. I had never seen a swimming pool before. The afternoon sunlight glittered off the water as if it were full of crystals. The sound system was tuned to a local radio station, which filled the air with the sound of cymbals, bongos, and tambourines.

My father was leaning against the bar dressed in white trousers and a pearly-white guayabera shirt. He was smoking a cigarette. The tobacco smoke mixed with the sun and salt.

When he saw us he placed his cigarette in an ashtray and opened his arms to me. He lifted me up. He smelled like lemons and Alberto VO5, which he creamed into his hair every morning to smooth it down.

He put me back down and gave my mother his arm and

walked her over to the bar where we sat on stools and looked out at the bay. He made my mother a margarita with a rim of salt around the glass. He stuck a small, red paper umbrella in her drink. My father concocted a fizzy pink drink with ginger ale and orange juice for me and placed a plastic stirrer inside the glass in the shape of a mermaid.

My parents looked handsome in their white clothes, which accentuated their dark skin. I thought that had been the happiest afternoon of my life until my mother and I got back on the bus to go home.

I knew it, she said as she rubbed her lipstick off with a couple of squares of toilet paper. Your father is having an affair with that waitress!

I knew exactly whom she was talking about.

My mother was very skinny. When she described herself she'd hold up her pinkie in the air and say, Skinny like a pinkie.

Her little finger would always be a symbol of her body to me.

The waitress had been wearing very tight clothes so her stomach bulged over her jeans and her thighs rubbed together as she walked. She was a beauty. My father always said a woman needs to be full. No matter how much my mother tried to fatten up, she couldn't. My father said that holding a skinny woman was like holding gristle and bone. He said that a real man wanted a body of pillows.

He never said, You, Rita, are gristle and bone, or You, Rita, need to fatten up, or You, Rita, are like a chicken wing. He was never that obvious in his cruelty.

The woman was wearing red flip-flops that were made with a plastic, two-inch heel. We would never forget those shoes.

I knew my mother was right. That woman was too nice

and that's a sure sign if there is any perfect sign at all. I was expecting her to pull out a piece of candy at any moment. Of course my father denied it.

As the bus rolled through the dark mountains along the windy road away from the bay and toward our house, I could feel the orange juice burn in my stomach and I began to feel dizzy. When we got off the bus, the high heels from my mother's shoes sank into the hot black asphalt that was like a lake of chewing gum. She had to lift her legs up high to pull her shoes out of the ooze.

That day marked the beginning of her anger. Her fury was a seed and it had been planted on that afternoon. By the time she shot Maria that seed had grown into a large tree that covered our lives with its shade of bile.

When my father came back home that night, he found that his clothes had been thrown out the front door and lay in a small pile on the damp, warm ground.

I lay in bed listening to them speak to each other in low whispers that were like screams.

You were something, my mother said. I thought she said.

Don't spill yourself, my father said. I thought he said.

Their angry whispers made broken words and sentences.

I will speak to God, my mother said. I thought she said.

In the morning my father was drinking his coffee by the stove. He was not wearing a shirt because all of his clothes were dumped outside. I knew his clothes would be covered in tiny black ants by now. He would have to shake the insects out and pluck them off.

Good morning, Ladydi, he said.

There was a huge welt on his shoulder surrounded by indentations. It was a human bite.

From then on my mother could no longer listen to love

songs. Before that night she'd been a songbird. The radio was on all the time and she'd sway, twirl, and spin to Juan Gabriel or Luis Miguel's songs as she cleaned the house, cooked, or ironed my father's white work shirts. From then on the radio was turned off and she just might as well have turned her happiness to off.

Love songs make me feel stupid, she said.

You're not stupid, Mama, I said.

The songs make me feel like I ate too much candy, Coke, ice cream, and cake. The songs make me feel like I've come home from a birthday party.

Once, when we were at Estefani's house, the radio turned to a love song. The melody filled the rooms. My mother panicked and ran out of the house to get away from the song. She threw up under a small orange tree. She threw up the melody, chords, the waltzes, and drums of love. It was pure green love bile on the green ground. I ran after her and held her hair away from her face as she vomited.

Your father killed the music for me, she said.

Being in Acapulco also made me think of the fortune-teller who told my mother the wrong fortune. Did her fortune include this event? Did the teller let her know she was going to shoot her daughter's sister?

I looked out the taxi window as we moved through the crowded streets toward the hospital. I looked out on T-shirt shops, taco stands, and restaurants.

Acapulco also reminded me of the time we had my mother's wedding band cut off by a locksmith. Most people in Guerrero did not wear rings. Hands and fingers swelled in the heat and, once a ring was on, it might never slip off.

After my father left us, my mother did not take her slim, gold wedding band off. It grew into her and became part of her finger, lost in the swollen flesh. On cool evenings, I could sometimes see the glimmer of gold in the lumpy skin as she cut up tomatoes or onions.

One day I watched as she spent most of the morning trying to remove the ring. She tried soap and cooking oil to make her finger slippery, but nothing worked.

After a few hours she said, We're going to go to Acapulco and get this damn ring cut off.

Yes, Mama.

If they can't cut it off, I'm cutting off my finger and that's that.

It wasn't until we were on the bus heading to Acapulco that I found out why she'd made this decision. Her biblical logic didn't surprise me. She'd had a dream.

My mother listened to her dreams as if she were Moses. She said most problems people had these days were because they did not listen and act on their dreams. If she'd had a dream that locusts were coming we'd have moved off of the mountain years ago. It's too bad that dream never came to her.

I've had a dream about my ring, she said.

The dream contained an important revelation.

If I don't get my wedding band off my finger, the birds will stop singing, she said. In the dream she was standing in the dark and parrots, canaries, and sparrows were standing on the branches of one orange tree. They all had their beaks wide open, but no sound emerged as the birds strained their necks back and looked up to heaven.

The locksmith cut the ring off of my mother's hand with a sharp file. It only took a second.

I've done this thousands of times, the locksmith said as he placed the ring, now cut into two pieces, in the palm of my mother's hand.

She looked down at the two commas of gold.

What the hell am I supposed to do with this? she said.

That locksmith did not know he had saved the songbirds of Mexico.

At the emergency room Maria's arm was sewn up and bandaged. The doctor said she'd been very lucky. The bullet had only fractured her arm.

It was my mother's unlucky lucky day.

As the doctors were taking care of Maria, her mother, Luz, arrived. This could only mean that my mother had told her.

I could not look at Luz.

I stared at the linoleum hospital floor.

I knew this was retribution. Luz was not going to press charges against my mother. Luz had it coming. How dare she fool around with her friend's husband? It was payback time and Luz was lucky her daughter was alive.

In the movies, my mother would have had a huge realization after shooting Maria, which would have made her quit drinking. In the movies, she would have dedicated her life to helping alcoholics or battered women. In the movies, God would have smiled at her repentance. But this was not the movies.

Eleven

At home my mother was lying in bed under a cotton sheet. The television was off. For the first time in years, I heard the deep, loud jungle silence. I heard crickets and I heard the mosquito swarms buzz around the house.

Her form under the white cloth looked like a boulder. On the floor, beside the bed, were three empty beer bottles. The brown glass of the empty containers looked like gold awash in the band of moonlight that came in from a window.

I sat at the edge of the bed.

I thought it was your father, my mother whimpered from inside her sheet-cave.

Go to sleep, Mama.

I really, really thought it was your father, she said again.

In the silent room I wanted to reach out and pick up the remote control and turn the television on.

I did not know what to do with this kind of quiet.

The sound of the TV had made me feel like we were having a party or it felt like we had a large family. The sound of the television was aunts and uncles and brothers and sisters.

The silence of a mother and daughter alone on a

mountain where a crime has been committed was the silence of the last two people on Earth.

I left my mother and went to my small room. I took off my T-shirt. It had Maria's blood on it. I took off my skirt and underwear that were stiff from dried urine and lay on my bed.

The notebook I'd taken along with Paula's photographs was still in the back pocket of my jeans that were laid out at the foot of my bed. I reached for it and sat on the bed and began to read. The handwriting belonged to Paula.

The notebook contained lists of things written with a blunt pencil. The first pages had lists of animals and animal parts. The rows itemized: two tigers, three lions, and one panther.

The next few pages had lists of women's names. Some of the names had last names and some did not. The list read: Mercedes, Aurora, Rebeca, Emilia, Juana, Juana Arrondo, Linda Gonzalez, Lola, Leona, and Julia Mendez.

The rest of the notebook was blank except for the last page where Paula's address was written: Chulavista, Guerrero, outside Chilpancingo, house of Concha.

I closed the notebook and placed it under my mattress with the photographs. Then I lay down on my bed and went to sleep.

The sound of the television woke me up. A bullfight was being broadcast from the great bullring in Mexico City.

I lay in bed listening. I could not understand why my mother was watching a bullfight as she'd sworn off them years ago. She'd seen a documentary where she learned that horses have their vocal cords severed and that is why they do not neigh, nicker, or scream during a bullfight. On our large, flat-screen television, we also could see that the bulls cry. On our mountain we saw their tears roll out of their eyes and fall on the sand that was stained with blood and sequins.

I stretched and walked out to the kitchen. My mother was at the kitchen table drinking a beer. She had a plate of toasted peanuts and garlic dusted with orange chili powder in front of her.

She looked up at me. I was afraid. I wanted to see the change. What was it going to be like? Who were we? Yellow beer tears stained her cheeks.

Paula was gone. Estefani was moving to Mexico City so her mother could get better medical care. Maria would never speak to me again. Ruth had been stolen forever. My father was over there.

That morning the mountain was empty.

I closed my hands into fists so that I would not start to count up the amount of people we had lost on my fingers.

My mother looked at me and took a swig of her beer. She looked different. If I could have sucked on her finger, as I used to do as a baby, it would not have tasted like mangoes and honey. Her finger would have tasted like those chicken wishbones turned from white bone to purple, which she used to place in a glass jar of vinegar so I could see how the brittle bone turned into rubber.

At the front door every insect on our mountain was still feeding on Maria's blood.

I knew if I walked out the door that trail of insects would lead me straight down the highway.

Mother, you didn't clean up, I said. You let the ants do it?

My mother looked at me with her new face.

I don't clean up blood, my mother said. It's not my thing.

After this day, my mother's neck was always bent to one side with her ear craned upward, listening for something. I knew she was listening for his Made in America cowboy boots to step out of a bus, step onto the boiling highway of asphalt, and swagger up the mountain to our home. He was going to say, You shot my daughter!

My mother sat at the kitchen table and looked at me.

Ladydi, she said, all this just proves that Maria came out of a goddamn Xerox machine!

Part Two

Twelve

The next day Mike picked me up on the side of the highway. He acted as if nothing had happened. It was as if my mother had not shot his sister. It was as if he were not picking me up in a red Mustang instead of boarding the bus to take me to my first job as a nanny to a young boy in Acapulco.

We'd made a date for nine in the morning and I thought he'd never get there. Passenger trucks tumbled past, covering me with dust and diesel fumes as an hour went by. Finally he rode up in the new red convertible and reached over, swung the door open, and gestured for me to get inside. He had his iPod earbuds stuck deep into his ears so he just gestured to get in the car.

His music was turned up so loud I could hear a soft beat coming out of the earbuds. We raced down the highway with him bopping his fingers on the steering wheel. At one point he turned and offered some Trident Cool Bubble chewing gum. He held up two fingers to say, Take two. I took two of the pieces, chewed it up hard, and blew small bubbles that crushed and broke open in my mouth as we moved down the road.

Mike steered with his knees as he lit a cigarette. He was

wearing a gold ring with a large diamond on his thumb. He had a tattoo of the letter Z on his pointer finger. The letter Z made everything quiet inside of me. Don't say anything; don't say anything, I said to myself. Z stands for the most dangerous drug cartel in Mexico. Everyone knows this.

Mike was not going to talk about what had happened to Maria. He was plugged into his iPod listening to rap and I was staring out the window at herds of goats. As I looked at him, I thought Maria did not belong to him. She did not even look like him. In that car, at that moment, I knew she was the one I loved most. I did not know this before, even when I held her broken arm in my arms.

Don't come back, my mother had said to me last night when she helped me pack up my few belongings. The woman who helped me pack was my new mother. I was still not exactly sure what form this newness would take. This was my after-she'd-shot-Maria mother. It was going to take some time to get to know each other.

Everyone's goal was to never come back. It used to be that there was a whole community that lived on this mountain, but that ended when they built the Sun Highway from Mexico City to Acapulco. My mother says that that highway cut our people in two pieces. It was like a machete that cut a body in half. Some people were left on one side of the black oily asphalt and some were left on the other. This meant that everyone had to continually cross the road back and forth. A passenger bus killed my mother's mother when she tried to cross the road to take her own mother, my great-grandmother, a jug of milk. On that day there was blood and white milk all over the road.

At least twenty people had been killed crossing the highway in the past years. Dogs, horses, chickens, and iguanas were hit too. Carcasses of snakes that had been run over also lined the highway like red and green streamers.

After my grandmother was hit, my mother kept her few belongings. My grandmother's party shoes are still in a shoebox under my mother's bed. They don't fit either of us, our feet are flat and our toes are spread wide from wearing plastic flip-flops our whole lives. The elegant shoes are made of blue satin with a pretty blue bow on the front. A famous actress gave the shoes to my grandmother; she swore it was Elizabeth Taylor. My grandmother worked as a cleaning lady at the Los Flamingos hotel which had belonged to Johnny Weissmuller, the actor who played Tarzan. All that is left from that old romantic Acapulco are those blue satin shoes under my mother's bed.

Ladydi, promise me you'll keep yourself ugly, my mother had said before I left in the morning.

At our kitchen table, which was an altar to beer, canned tuna fish, ants, potato chips, and prepackaged donuts dusted in icing sugar, I promised her I would never wear lipstick or perfume and that I would not grow out my hair, but keep it short and boyish.

Just keep in the shade, don't walk in the sun, she said.

Yes, Mama.

I wondered if I should bring Paula's photos and her notebook with me and finally placed them in my bag. I knew if I left them here the jungle insects would chew them up or the humidity would soon cover them with mould.

The construction of the highway was the beginning of the destruction of our families. People began to leave because they needed jobs and so many people went to the United States. My grandfather and my mother's two brothers and their families all moved to San Diego. They departed after my grandmother was run over. They never wanted to look over their shoulder and so we never heard from them again. My mother said the drug traffickers finally destroyed our mountain. No community can survive so many tragedies.

All that was left on our mountain were a few women who still knew how to cook an iguana wrapped in avocado leaves.

As Mike drove me down the road toward the Pacific Ocean the air conditioning felt nice and cool on my face.

As we moved down the highway I looked at the pink stone of our mountain that had been cut to make way for the road. It seemed exposed like scraped, raw skin.

Thirteen

Halfway to Acapulco, Mike turned off the highway and onto a dirt road. I looked at him, but he was so lost inside his iPod I thought he'd forgotten I was with him. I looked out the window and thought of my mother living alone on the mountain drinking beer and watching television and felt so ashamed of myself because I knew that all I wanted to do on this big, round blue planet was find my father.

The speed of the car picked up a dust cloud around us. I thought we were like those television car commercials where the vehicle veers off the road and onto rough terrain to show how it can go anywhere. In the commercial Mike and I would be a couple wearing dark glasses and tight jeans. My frizzy hair would be blown out and cascading down my back.

We drove for about twenty minutes through a road lined by palm trees until we reached a dilapidated shack with a yellow hammock swinging between two trees.

A tall, bald man walked out of the shack as Mike turned off the engine. The man stood and did not walk toward us.

Mike pulled the earbuds out.

Stay in here and be pretty and don't leave the car, Mike said.

The man was so skinny his jeans settled on his hips and a streak of brown skin was exposed between his blue T-shirt and belt. His hip bones stood out and made deep shadows on both sides of his body. He was also barefoot and wore a wide straw hat that was frayed and worn.

He held a machine gun pointed straight at us.

What are we doing here? I said to Mike in a whisper as if the man could hear us out there.

Don't move.

What are we doing here?

Quiet. Quiet.

Mike got out of the car and held out his hand to the man in a gesture that said stop.

She's my sister, Mike said aloud. Hey, don't worry, man. She's blind.

The man looked at me and back at Mike.

She's blind. Yes, yes. She was born blind.

The man lowered his machine gun.

Mike turned and pointed something at me and I heard the car lock. It was the car's remote control that not only locked me in the convertible, but also locked the windows.

Mike and the man went inside the shack.

There were three black Escalades parked to the right of the shack in the shade of several palm trees. There were also two Rottweilers tied to the fender of one of these SUVs with leather straps. The dogs were panting hard in the heat and their dark red tongues hung out of their mouths.

On the fleshy elongated leaves of a maguey cactus two little-girl dresses dried in the sun. One dress was white and the other was blue.

As each minute passed it seemed to me that the world became more and more quiet. The hum of insects even disappeared as I began to bake inside the hot, locked car.

The dresses drying on the maguey cactus made me think of the narrow twig arms of a little girl coming out of the sleeves. The garments were almost dry and they lifted and blew in the heat.

On the ground beside the cactus there was a toy bucket and a toy broom.

The Trident Cool Bubble chewing gum had lost its pink, circus cotton-candy flavor.

My mind wandered in the hot-car-daydream.

With the motor and the air conditioning off, and the windows closed shut, all the air was sucked up and used by my body. My thighs were wet through my jeans and I was moist all over. I felt thirsty and dizzy and almost drugged by the heat. I imagined a mirage of white seagulls flying above the shack, the Rottweilers, and the skinny man. In my stifling daydream I thought birds were clouds and I imagined a little girl in a white dress picking up seagull feathers from the ground.

At some point, I could not tell if I'd been locked in the car for ten minutes or two hours. I was pulled awake when the dogs began to bark as Mike came out of the shack.

Mike walked toward the car. He took out his car keys from his jeans, pointed the remote control, and I heard the locks flip open under the windows. He walked quickly with his face bent down against the sun. He opened the car door and slid inside.

What happened? I asked.

Did you fall asleep?

Who was that man?

Roll down the window.

Mike placed a small plastic bag on the seat between us.

He turned on the engine, turned the car around and we drove back down the dirt road toward the highway.

Mike beat his fingers on the steering wheel to some hip-hop music in his mind.

He was sweating and drops fell from his hair down the back of his neck. He held the car's steering wheel between his knees and pulled off his shirt with a practiced swoop over his head.

The number 25 was tattooed on his upper arm beside a dark red rose. As I sat beside him, I could smell that flower. I could smell the rose on his arm as if I were leaning over a rose bush and smelling the soft petals.

So why did they call you Ladydi, anyway? Was it just because your mother liked that princess so much? Mike asked.

No, Mike.

I was not going to tell him that my mother named me Ladydi because she hated what Prince Charles had done to Diana.

Thanks to our television, my mother knew the whole story inside out. She loved any woman to whom a man had been unfaithful. It was a special sisterhood of pain and hatred. She used to say that, if there were a saint for betrayed women, that saint would be Lady Diana. One day, on the Biography Channel, my mother learned that Prince Charles claimed he had never loved her.

Why didn't he just lie? my mother said. Why didn't he just lie?

I was not named Ladydi after Diana's beauty and fame. I was named Ladydi because of her shame. My mother said that Lady Diana had lived the true Cinderella story: closets full of broken glass slippers, betrayal, and death.

For one birthday I was given a plastic Princess Diana

doll wearing a tiara. My father had brought it for me from the United States. In fact, over the years he bought me several Princess Diana dolls.

My name was my mother's revenge. It was a kind of philosophy to her. She did not value forgiveness. In her revenge philosophy there were all kinds of scenarios. For example, the person you were avenging did not need to know about the acts of revenge as in the case of my father and my name.

When people who met me were surprised at my name, and said it aloud a few times over very sweetly, I could almost taste grains of sugar in my mouth. I knew that they were comparing my face to Diana's face and feeling sorry for me. They were measuring my darkness against her fairness.

On the outskirts of Acapulco Mike had to drive down a long tunnel, which cut through the middle of the last mountain before the bay. I'd been inside this tunnel many times in buses and taxis.

As we drove out of the dark tunnel, the bright ocean sunlight filled the car.

Mike's light blue jeans were splattered with blood.

Now I knew that blood could smell like roses.

My mother once saw a documentary on how the Zetas turn people into killers. She said that they tied a man's hands behind his back and forced him to kneel and eat his own vomit, or eat someone else's vomit.

Mike and I drove through the city streets toward the old section of Acapulco where rundown mansions from the 1940s and 1950s had been abandoned. In recent years, people had begun to buy up these properties and fix them. The houses were built into the mountainside, into the rock, above the Caleta and Caletilla beaches. From here there was a view of the bay on the left and Roqueta Island straight ahead. To the right one could see way out to the open ocean.

You know, Mike said, to this day your father sends my mother money.

What?

Yes, to this day your father sends my mother money.

I don't believe you. He hasn't sent us money for years.

Well, he sends my mother money. Every month.

Please say this isn't true. It can't be.

Okay. It isn't true.

Where does he live? Where does the money come from?

New York City.

Mike pulled up to a large house painted in new white paint and dropped me off at the front door.

Go on, he said. This is the place. Get out.

He dropped me at the front door and didn't even get out of the car. One forgets about manners when you've killed someone.

I obeyed. I knew to obey a killer. I obeyed when he gave me the plastic bag he'd carried out of the shack and placed between us in the Mustang. I obeyed when he told me to hold on to it until he needed it. I obeyed and placed it inside my black duffel bag with its broken zipper. I obeyed. I obeyed. I obeyed.

Mike rolled down his car window.

I'll be back to pick that bag up in a few days, he said.

Okay.

Don't steal anything.

I don't steal.

You're your mother's daughter.

Shut up!

I rang the doorbell. Mike drove off. He did not wait to see if anyone opened the door for me.

After a minute or two, a servant dressed in a pale pink uniform with a crisp, clean white apron opened the door. Her straight gray hair was braided with green ribbons and pinned up so it rested like a headband or crown above her forehead. She was about seventy years old and had brown-red skin and small, light brown eyes. I thought she looked like a squirrel.

I was also standing in front of a ghost, or what my mother called a Mexico ghost. This is the term my mother used for anything that was ancient. Over the years, my mother and I only had to say ghost and we knew exactly what we meant. A ghost could be in a basket, a tree, the taste of a tortilla, and even a song.

She spoke softly and told me that the family who lived there had been away for over a week. She did not know when they'd be back. Her name was Jacaranda. As I walked behind her into the house, she smelled like coconut oil and oranges.

Jacaranda explained that the home belonged to the Domingo family, which consisted of Mr Luis Domingo, Mrs Rebeca Domingo, and their six-year-old boy, Alexis.

As Jacaranda walked me through the house I could feel my mother walking beside me. I could almost hear her spit on the white leather sofas with matching white leather throw pillows; spit on the glass tables that had bronze statues of ballerinas balanced on square stands; spit on the cold marble floor; and spit on the white tile kitchen floor and stainless-steel sink.

I could hear her say, This is all too clean, it hurts. And, as I looked around, I knew she was going to ask me to describe everything. She would want to know what I could steal and bring back to her. She would have looked at this house and said, We need to say a prayer for some dirt.

The living-room windows opened on a garden, which was set on a cliff that looked out over the ocean. There was a life-sized bronze statue of a horse under a large bougainvillea tree. To one side of the garden there was a swimming pool made of light blue tiles and carved from the ground in the shape of a turtle.

Jacaranda opened the glass door and led me out into the garden and down a path toward the servants' rooms. We each had our own bedroom, but we shared a bathroom.

My bedroom contained a single bed and a chair and one small window that looked into the garage. The room smelled of a harsh, floral cleaning liquid. I looked out my window and could see a white Mercedes-Benz convertible and a black Escalade parked side by side in the garage.

Jacaranda told me I would have to wear a uniform also, like hers. She told me to change and instructed me to go to the kitchen once I was settled in so that she could make me some lunch.

I unpacked my few belongings and hid Paula's photographs and notebook and Mike's plastic bag under my mattress. There was no place else to keep them in the small room.

My cell phone rang. It was my mother.

I knew she stood at the clearing with her arm held up high in the air, trying to catch a signal. Her upper arm was burning from holding the phone up in the air and the effort of moving it back and forth between both hands.

It's terrible there, right? she said.

Yes. It's a filthy place.

Are you serious? What's it like?

It's fine.

But you do hate it?

Yes, I hate it.

The lies went back and forth between us. The truth was I already loved the clean house full of sea breeze and my mother wanted me back home immediately.

Stick it out, give it a chance, and stay.

Yes, I'll try, Mama.

You can always come home if you don't like it there.

The phone went dead. This always happened and meant that you had to dial back again and again. We all knew it was the reason Carlos Slim, the man who owned the phone company, was the richest man in the world. He made sure everyone in Mexico always had to call back.

What are you going to do? my mother used to say. Stop calling your family? Stop calling the doctor? Stop calling whomever it might be who might, just might, help you find a stolen daughter? Of course we all call back!

I turned off my phone and went to the kitchen. I walked across the cool white tiled floor in my red plastic flip-flops from the jungle.

Jacaranda was making tortillas filled with cheese and raw green chilies on the stove and told me to sit down at the breakfast table. From the kitchen there was a view of the bay.

The table was set with three places. There were even three individual salt- and pepper-shakers next to tall crystal glasses of lemonade filled with slivers of lemon rind.

Jacaranda took an ice tray out of the freezer and dropped star-shaped ice cubes into our drinks.

She placed two tortillas on a plate in front of me and sat down. She had to squeeze in between the chair and glass table.

Once you've had babies, she explained, your stomach always wants to go back to that size as if it longs to have the baby back, she said.

Jacaranda placed her hands on her stomach and said with pride, I had eleven children.

As I ate she told me that she'd worked at this house for the past eight years. Before that she'd been a cleaning lady in a hotel for over forty years.

After you've worked in a hotel, there's nothing about human nature you don't know.

I listened to her as I ate the tortillas.

Most people are kind, she explained, and most women are unfaithful to their men.

I told her that my mother would dispute this information.

No, Jacaranda insisted. There is only one thing no one understands. Men get caught and women don't.

Jacaranda also told me how people steal everything from hotel rooms, even light bulbs.

I knew this, of course. My mother had stolen light bulbs all the time.

Jacaranda remembered her very first job was to walk the streets, knock on doors, and ask poor women if they wanted to sell their braids. She would buy each braid for ten pesos back in those days. Sometimes the women would cut off their long braid or ponytail right then and there so Jacaranda always carried a sharp scissor with her. Most of the time the braids were in boxes or bags in the women's closets and drawers.

This was before everyone was making synthetic hair and bringing it in from China, she explained. This was when women still had long hair.

Most people don't have really, really long hair anymore.

Yes, women used to grow their hair down to their knees. I worked for a woman here in Acapulco who had a small wig company. The hair that was bought from going door-to-door was laid out in three categories: short, medium and long. Then the hair was disinfected and dyed and made into wigs and hairpieces. These hairpieces were very fashionable and were sold in Mexico City at a shop in the center of town.

Do you still have any of this hair? I asked.

No. But I used to imagine the rich ladies in Mexico dancing at parties and wearing the hair of a barefoot Nahua Indian from Guerrero.

One memorable day Jacaranda bought ten braids from one house alone. These were the braids from five generations of women. The colors ranged from black to gray to white.

All the braids were as long as my arm, Jacaranda remembered.

It's hard to imagine.

I used to embroider with my own hair. I used it as thread, Jacaranda said.

My mother still uses her own hair to sew on a button or fix a hem.

Yes, I used to do that too.

Does someone else live here? I asked, pointing to the third place set at the table.

Yes. Julio, the gardener. He didn't show up today, but will be back tomorrow.

After lunch Jacaranda gave me a tour of the house.

As we walked through the rooms, Jacaranda chewed on little pieces of paper. The white pulp appeared between her teeth every now and again. Jacaranda said she developed this habit as a girl as her mother was too poor to buy her chewing gum. She wanted her friends to think she was chewing real gum and it turned into a habit.

Every room seemed unlived in. The floors were so clean I knew I could drop a slice of an apple or a piece of toast on the floor and just pick it up and eat it. My skin was dirtier than the floor. There was no crumb for an ant and no spider for a scorpion. There were no cobwebs. And there was nothing personal in the house like a jacket hanging over the back of a chair or a rolled-up magazine on a table or photograph displayed in a frame.

The master bedroom had a king-sized bed that faced a huge window that looked over the garden and out over the ocean. There was wooden figure of Jesus on the cross hanging on the wall above the bed. The room led off into one large bathroom that had a Jacuzzi in the center of the room and a massage table.

One door in the bedroom was closed and we didn't look inside. Jacaranda explained that was the dressing room where they kept their clothes.

That door is locked, she said.

Next to the bedroom was the boy's room.

He's little and does not go to school yet, Jacaranda explained. You'll have to play with him.

This was the one room that looked lived in. There were toys everywhere, piled on every surface and all over the floor. There were at least thirty stuffed animals thrown on the bed like a pile of pillows. On one chest of drawers there were three large glass jars filled with candy. The red, yellow, and green M&Ms shone in the Acapulco sun.

The boy's bed was carved in the shape of a whale.

The next room Jacaranda showed me was the television room. It had a wall-to-wall television screen so it was like a movie theater. In front of the screen were two sofas, three armchairs and two large beanbag chairs. One wall was covered from floor to ceiling with a collection of DVDs.

This is what they love to do. They watch movies and eat popcorn or hot dogs. They can watch the same movie over and over again, Jacaranda said.

I had seen the house on television.

I had never walked on a marble floor before, which was like walking on a piece of ice, but I had seen it. I had never sat down at a perfectly set table, with two forks, two knives, a soup spoon, and an ironed linen napkin, but I had seen it. I had never used a saltshaker or looked at star-shaped ice cubes in my glass, but I had seen it.

I knew then that I could go to the Pyramids in Egypt and they'd be familiar. I was sure I could ride a horse or drive a jeep on a safari in Africa. I knew how to cook lasagne and lasso a calf.

I remembered some of the violence and catastrophes I'd watched on television that had helped to build my television-knowledge.

When I thought of this, I tasted sour milk in my mouth like milk that sat out on the table in the jungle heat for too long. Yes, a flood could feel familiar. Yes, a car crash could feel familiar. I thought yes, a rape could feel familiar. Yes, I could be dying and even the deathbed would be familiar.

Then I thought of Mike at that ranch and the blood splattered on his clothes and I knew what had happened even though I had not been inside that broken-down shack.

I'd seen my life on television.

Fourteen

The first night in my servant's room I lay in bed and looked at the tiny window that opened onto the large garage and the cars. There was nothing else to look at.

A smell of gasoline filled my room. It was like sleeping in a Pemex gas station.

I knew that I didn't have to worry about insects. The house smelled like rotten lemons from constant fumigations.

That night there was one question that would not let go of me. I wondered if Maria knew by now. They must have told her that this was the reason God punished her with a harelip. It was the curse for her mother's infidelity with my father. Someone must have told her the truth and explained why my mother shot her.

Was Maria looking in the mirror and seeing my daddy's face all over her face?

I wanted to know if what Mike said was true and if my father sent Maria's mother money. If my mother ever found this out, she would find him. She would. The time of hunger for him would be over.

I thought of all these things as I lay on the mattress where I'd hidden Paula's photos and her notebook and Mike's plastic bag with a brick of heroin in it.

A brick made fifty bags.

Fifteen

The very next morning Julio, the gardener, walked through the front door and I fell in love.

He walked right into my body.

He climbed up my ribs and into me. I thought to myself, Say a prayer for ladders.

I wanted to smell his neck and place my mouth on his mouth and taste him and hold him. I wanted to smell the smell of garden and grass and palm tree, smell of rose and leaf and lemon flower. I fell in love with the gardener and his name was Julio.

I spent the morning following him around the garden. He trimmed, dug, and cut. He rubbed the leaves of a lemon tree between his fingers and smelled them. He took a few flat silver seeds out of the back pocket of his jeans and pressed them into the dirt. He used long shears to cut the grass.

After an hour, he left and went to get a ladder from the garage so that he could cut the pink bougainvillea that grew along one wall and beside the life-sized bronze horse. As he snipped at the overgrown branches, yellow pollen was shaken into the air and the flowers, like paper flowers, covered the ground.

Julio was in his early twenties. His skin was deeply tanned from working in the sun all day. He had a short Afro that stood up like a black crown above him and light brown eyes.

Julio was kind to the flowers and the leaves. He cupped the roses with his hands as if he was honored to hold them. He twirled vines between his fingers as if they were locks of hair. He walked gently on the grass as if he did not want the small blades to break or even bend under his weight.

Plants in my life had always been something to fight against. Trees were filled with tarantulas. Vines strangled everything. Large red ants lived under roots and snakes hid near the prettiest flowers. I also knew to stay away from the unusual dry brown patches of jungle that were suffocating from the herbicide dropped by the helicopters. That poison would continue to burn through the land for decades. Everyone on my piece of mountain always dreamed of the city and all that cement where no insect survived. We could never imagine why anyone would want a garden.

Because I loved Julio, the cars and trucks outside on the street sounded like rivers. The diesel smokc from passenger buses smelled like flowers and the rotten five-day-old garbage by the front door smelled sweet. Cement walls became mirrors. My small ugly hands turned into starfish.

In those hours that I followed Julio around the garden, he never spoke to me.

After Julio left each day, I sat in my room and prayed. I prayed that the beautiful garden of bougainvillea trees, roses, bowers, lemon and magnolia trees would dry up and that the lawn would become overgrown with weeds.

I prayed that Julio would have to come to the house every day to take care of his sick garden.

Very late, after I had fallen asleep, my cell phone rang. It was my mother. She was furious.

I did not know if she was drunk or not but I did know she was standing alone in the dark up on the clearing and screaming into her phone. The connection was poor. I started to yell also as if my voice could reach her across the city streets and over the mountain, down the highway and up into her ear.

Between the bad connection and her screams, I could not understand what she was calling about.

What are you doing all alone up there on Delphi? It's late. It's dark. Go home! I cried.

You stole it! You took it and you didn't even ask my permission!

What did I take?

Don't give me that! You know what you took!

What?

You get on a bus and bring it back right now!

This conversation went back and forth and finally we were cut off. I never understood what it was she thought I'd stolen. She did not call back.

I closed my eyes and imagined what happened next. My mother cursed and turned off her phone. She plunged down the mountain toward our little house with her toes craned over the front of her flip-flops, hanging onto the plastic soles like a parrot's talons to a branch. I could see her stumble and slip.

I prayed there was no moon, it was the darkest night ever, she was lost and a scorpion had stung her hand as she stumbled against a tree. The backward prayer was never backward enough.

When I'd arrived, Jacaranda gave me two uniforms to wear. So, like her, I dressed in a pink dress with a white apron over the uniform.

The next morning when I went into the kitchen Jacaranda was already up and making coffee. She offered me a plate of scrambled eggs with slices of hot dogs in them.

I asked her when our employers were coming back, but she had no idea. She said they were only supposed to have gone away for the weekend to visit relatives in Nogales, in the state of Sonora.

As the morning unfolded, Jacaranda told me about the family we were working for.

Mr Domingo owned a ranch in Coahuila, very north, right across from the border at Laredo. The ranch was known for its huge white-tailed bucks. All the animals were harvested on his property.

Last January Jacaranda went to the ranch for the first time. There was a large fenced-in field filled with deer to one side of the ranch house. Behind the house there were cages that contained old lions and tigers that Mr Domingo would buy from zoos.

Rich people from the United States liked to hunt there, Jacaranda said. A deer cost you two thousand dollars to kill.

It seems so little.

Little? Who knows? The birds were free. The monkeys were free too.

They had monkeys?

Nobody wanted to kill monkeys, she said.

Oh, really? Why?

Why kill something that's free?

While she'd been there, a group of businessmen from Texas had hired the ranch for a hunt.

The large living room at the ranch house contained a polar bear rug and dozens of deer heads on the walls. The wide, circular bar stools were made of elephant feet. The lamps were made of deer legs that had been hollowed out with a long drill so that the electrical wires could be threaded through.

Jacaranda said that Mr Domingo liked to go hunting in Africa once a year and that, while she worked there, two large trunks arrived at the house with dead animals in them that lay flat like clothes and that were later stuffed.

It was Jacaranda's job to clean the glass eyes of all the animals in the room.

Mr Domingo likes the eyes to look real and shine, she said.

Twice a week Jacaranda had to fill a bucket with water and bleach and, using a rag and standing on a ladder, she'd clean the glass eyes so that they would shine with life. She said that she would look to see the hole where the bullet had entered the animal, but that the skins were sewn so perfectly, she could never tell.

Jacaranda described Mrs Domingo as a nice woman from an old family that came from Sonora. She was refined and elegant and her husband was not. Mrs Domingo hated living in Acapulco and Jacaranda said that she fought with Mr Domingo all the time about wanting to leave here. Mrs Domingo spent most of her time watching movies.

She does not like to go shopping or go to the beauty parlor like other women. She just stays home and watches movies and plays with her son, Jacaranda said. In any case, Mr Domingo does not like them to leave the house.

Mr Domingo was born in Acapulco and his father, who died a few years ago, owned a small hotel, which was the one that Jacaranda had worked in years ago.

This is how I ended up here. I'd already worked for the family at the hotel cleaning the rooms.

After we finished breakfast, I went out into the garden to wait for Julio's arrival so I could follow him around and watch him work.

From the garden I could look out over the ocean and, on that day, I saw two large cruise ships come into the harbor. Several small boats from one of the docks motored out to the ships to pick up passengers and bring them into Acapulco to go shopping.

When Julio arrived, I followed him around and watched him work. He was very quiet and accepted my adoration. I didn't know how to act any other way. I loved him and wanted him and no one had ever prepared me for this devotion.

I longed for an order, for him to say, Bring me a glass of water.

I wished he'd say, Hold my shears while I move the ladder.

I wanted to be given instructions.

I wanted to obey him.

I wanted to kneel.

We walked in the silent garden and fell in love to the sound of things being trimmed and planted.

Every day Jacaranda and I got up, bathed, and dressed in our pink uniforms with the clean, white aprons. She wore white plastic nurse shoes, while I wore my old plastic flip-flops.

Every day we'd groom for the arrival of our employers. Every day we'd clean the clean house and Julio would scoop the leaves out of the swimming pool with a long net.

The money Jacaranda had been given to run the house and buy food was slowly used up. We ate everything in the larder. One day we made a meal of caviar wrapped up in tortillas served with a hot tomato sauce.

We never touched the bottles of champagne or cases of wine.

One day Jacaranda, Julio, and I were sitting in the kitchen drinking lemonade together when Jacaranda said, I have to tell you both something I confirmed yesterday.

What is it? Julio asked.

We have all suspected this, but now I know. No one is ever coming back to this house. They were all killed on a highway outside Nogales months ago.

No one will ever show up again, Julio said.

Was the boy killed too? I asked.

That's what they said on the news. It took this long to confirm their identities. They had many.

We all knew there were empty houses all over Mexico that no one ever came home to.

I'm going to stay, Jacaranda said, while I look for another job.

Me too, Julio said.

Me too, I answered.

Julio was content to have me follow him around. He still did the gardening because he said he only did it out of respect for the garden anyway. I'd hold his shears for him and it was as if I held his hand. The bags of dead leaves, the ladder, the shears, the rake, and the net for the swimming pool became parts of his body to me.

One day I followed him to the garage. He needed to get some fertilizer to sprinkle under the magnolia tree. The bags of fertilizer were kept in there in stacks beside an enormous tank of gasoline that even had a fuel pump, just like the ones at gas stations.

One match, one small spark, only one match, could

blow up the house, Julio said as I followed him into that dark, hot garage.

In the garage, Julio walked into me. The weight of his body pressed me against the door of the Mercedes and I could feel the door handle in the small of my back.

Julio twisted me to one side and opened the car door and pushed me backward until I lay on the car seat with my legs hanging out of the door. The car smelled like leather and perfume. Julio pushed my pink uniform from my thighs up to my waist and then rolled my underwear down my legs. I heard my flip-flops fall off my feet and onto the floor.

After that day, Julio moved into the house. He spent the morning in the garden. He trimmed plants and mowed the lawn or placed chemicals in the swimming pool. In the afternoon we watched movies.

At first we slept in my small servant's room in my narrow single bed but, after only a few days, we moved up to the master bedroom where we took baths in the Jacuzzi and slept in the king-sized bed. Jacaranda didn't mind because by this time she was living in the child's bedroom and sleeping in the whale-shaped bed.

In the bathroom I liked to look into every drawer of Mrs Domingo's vanity table. In one drawer she had at least fifty lipsticks. In another drawer she had over twenty different perfume bottles. I tried everything. I would cover my body with an orchid cream and used one cream on my knees and elbows that was made with gold dust. I also wore her Chanel No. 5 perfume.

Under the sink I found a box of jewelry. It was unlocked and hidden inside a towel. The box had two thick gold necklaces in it, a gold Rolex watch, and a ring with a very large diamond. I placed the jewel on my ring finger and it fit perfectly. I never took it off.

Now that we were lovers, Julio talked to me and I learned about his life. He had a strange way of talking. He said everything two or three times, but always in a different way. I slowly understood the rhythm of his talk, which I imagined was the way people spoke in the north of Mexico.

I'm just wayward, he said. What can I tell you? I was caught in the river like a rat. A rat-in-the-river-caught kind of man. Yes. I broke the life out of someone. I'm wayward.

He called me Princess Ladydi.

You're a one-and-only, he said. I'd shine my shoes for you and stand in the rain for five hours for you. Just you, Princess Ladydi.

I decided not to tell him why my mother named me after Lady Diana because I did not want to break my own heart.

I crossed the river but I was caught on the riverbank and the guard who guarded over me and watched me looked away and opened the way for me, Julio said.

Julio killed a US Border Patrol guard. This was why he was a gardener in Acapulco and not a gardener in California.

Julio used to work on Mr Domingo's ranch and grew up in Nuevo Laredo. When he killed the border guard he came back to Mexico. Mr Domingo helped him get out fast and got him as far away from the US border as possible. He gave Julio a job as a gardener in his own house in Acapulco. Julio said that there was nothing Mr Domingo hated more than the United States Border Patrol.

I needed to live as if I'd drowned in the river; I needed to appear to disappear and fill with water, float out to sea. Every US border guard thinks I drowned in the Rio Grande, Rio Bravo, Julio said.

Now I understood why Jacaranda did not interfere with

us. Julio had killed someone with his hands. She knew Julio held that border guard's neck and twisted and tore it like a young tree branch.

For six months we lived in the house together waiting for something to happen. This waiting reminded me of what it felt like when I was sick as a child and days and days went by without knowing when I would go back to school. Once I lay in a hammock with a high fever. For days my mother rocked that hammock and fanned the flies off my body until her arm must have ached. On my mountain, fanning flies off of someone is one of the kindest, most loving things a person can do for another. It really bothered me when I'd see documentaries on the television where flies were drinking the water from children's eyes in Africa. No one shooed them away, not even the person filming. That NatGeo cameraperson just filmed those flies drinking tears.

Once, when I told Julio I was tired of being locked in the house, he planned a day trip for us.

This was the first time I'd left the house since my arrival. I changed out of my servant's uniform and into my jeans and a T-shirt. I had not worn these clothes since the day I'd arrived with Mike. I could feel that my body was different inside my old clothes. It was a combination of walking on marble instead of dirt paths, sleeping in cold air under piles of blankets, and being loved by Julio night after night.

We walked down the hill from the marble house to Caleta beach.

Julio held my hand as we walked. You're my little girl, he said. Don't let go of my hand.

He liked to treat me like a child. I expected him to take a tissue out of his pocket and wipe my nose. He acted like he was taking me to the candy store. I loved to be his little baby and so I skipped at his side and forgot that he was a killer.

Julio bought the tickets for our ride across the bay to Roqueta Island in a glass-bottom boat. The truth is he did not want me to see the sand and ocean or the island. He did not want me to see the island's zoo with the old lion whose roar crossed the bay and could be heard on windless mornings. Julio wanted me to see the bronze statue of the Virgin of Guadalupe that was in the water, drowned in the sea. She was called the Virgin of the Sea.

Now you will see the mother of the water, he said. She protects the shipwrecked and fishermen. The drowned too.

The boat sat low in the water as if it were a wide canoe. Julio and I leaned over and looked through the glass that allowed us to see everything that moved under the boat. After a while we saw her shape beneath the waves.

The undersea world looked green through the boat's tinted glass. The virgin was bottle green in the green light with a crown on her head. She was surrounded by fish. There were sea snails on her shoulders. She was also a wishing well. There were coins around her on the ocean floor that glittered and gleamed silver in the sanctuary.

As we swayed above her, Julio said, We'd better pray. He bowed his head and folded his hands together.

The more I enter the more I find; and the more I find the more I seek, he said aloud. Amen. Amen.

You pray aloud?

Are you going to pray? he asked.

Later that night in the king-sized bed, Julio held me in his arms.

I had to show you that I'm drowned, drowned just like

her, like Mary, sleeping in the sea all night long in the dark dark, he said. Everyone thinks I'm at the bottom of the river. My mother thinks so too. It's too dangerous for me to be alive. I cannot dream at night. There's a big difference between living in the dark with a candle and living in the dark with a flashlight. I have a flashlight but I want a candle.

Your mother also thinks you're dead?

Yes. Everyone is praying for me.

Can't you let her know? She needs to know you're here.

My family is remembering that I was the fastest runner and the best jumper. I won every race. I was always the winner. I should have outrun that border guard. I didn't see him or hear him. My mother is saying, Julio would never, ever be caught. He'd rather drown. And I did. You love a drowned man, Princess Ladydi. When you kiss me do you taste the river? There's a cross for me, a white cross, where I was crossing.

With your name on it? I ask.

For the US police that white wood cross is the best proof that I'm dead. It's in my FBI file. Imagine that a riverside wood cross with plastic flowers actually proves to the FBI that my family thinks I'm dead.

With your name on it?

My name is not Julio.

From the master bedroom's bay window in the marble house we could see past the garden and large bronze horse, to the bay glittering with night lights. When I looked out after our day trip, I knew a virgin lived under that blue water.

Since I was a person who had never experienced cold weather, I loved to close the door and windows and turn up the air conditioning until the room was freezing. My teeth chattered. My teeth seemed almost to break against each other. I had never felt that kind of cold before. I loved it. I even loved the pain.

This room is the North Pole! Julio said.

He never asked me to turn the air conditioning off.

I would gather up all the blankets I could find from around the house and pile them on the bed. I had never slept in a cold room under blankets.

This is because you grew up in the jungle, Julio said. I grew up close to the desert where it can get very cold.

At night, in our Acapulco igloo, Julio told me his philosophy.

Life is a crazy, out of order, inside out, salt mixed with sugar place where the drowned can be walking on dry land, he said. Like the best outlaws, I know I'm going to die young. I don't even think about old age. It's not even in my imagination.

You have tamed me, I answered. I picked up his hand from the pillow and cuffed it around my wrist.

Julio thought people could be divided into day and night people. He said words could be divided this way also. Ugly night words, according to him, were words like rabies and nausea. Pretty night words were words like moon and milk and moth.

When Julio and I moved around under the blankets sparks of electricity crackled and lit up our bed.

Never had we seen anything like this before, only in the sky.

We would make love in the wool blanket lightning.

Sixteen

My mother's phone calls always brought news from our mountain. Estefani and her siblings never returned from Mexico City after their mother Augusta died from AIDS. Sofia, Estefani's grandmother, who'd run the OXXO by the Pemex gas station, had packed up and left to go and care for her orphaned grandchildren.

My mother told me that Paula and her mother had really disappeared. No one ever heard anything about them again.

I also knew that Maria's gunshot had healed and that she and her mother were still on our mountain.

I have a case of the misery, my mother said.

Oh, Mama. Please don't tell me.

I'm all wrong inside.

This meant she missed me, but she'd never say it.

Some mornings Julio and I would go out to the garden and spend the whole day there.

He'd lift me up onto the bronze horse and I would ride it.

Seventeen

Seven months went by in the empty marble house.

One day my mother called. She was angry. She said she'd been trying to call for days.

Why haven't you answered your phone? she asked. Damn, I've called and called! So you've forgotten about me? Is that what you've done?

I'm here.

If I had not reached you today, I was going to go straight to Acapulco.

Please, calm down. Why do you exaggerate? We talked a week ago.

Something has happened. Nothing happens here and now something happens, she said.

What?

Listen.

I'm listening, Mama.

Can you hear me?

Yes, I hear you fine.

Mike's been arrested. He's being taken to Mexico City.

Why to Mexico City?

They say he killed a man. They say he killed a little girl!

What?

Mike says that you were with him. You were on a bus.

I remembered. A girl's dresses were drying in the sun on the maguey pads. There were seagull feathers on the ground.

I could not even swallow my saliva, it just sat in my mouth, growing and growing, until I had to spit it out into my hand.

Mike says that you were with him. You were on a bus.

I held the phone in one hand and the gob of my saliva in the cup of my other hand.

You need to come here right away, she said. They want you in Mexico City to give your testimony. Mike says you can clear him. It will be quick. Tell them the truth! He says you know what happened.

I had a dream in that car. I was with Maria, my dear sister who looked just like my father. In my dream I called her sister, little sister. My dream told me she was the one I loved the most. I had not known this before, even when I held her broken, bloody arm in my arms. The word sister in my dream woke me up as if I'd been awoken by the sound of a firecracker or bullet in the air. The word cracked me awake. White seagulls flew above the shack and the Rottweiler and the skinny man. Maybe the birds were clouds. Maybe the clouds were birds. A little girl in a white dress picked up the feathers from the ground. Mike's red-rose tattoo filled the car with rose perfume. I obeyed him when he told me to keep the heroin for him. I obeyed and placed the brick of heroin inside my black bag with its broken zipper. I obeyed.

I can't hear you anymore, Mama. I'll call you back.

I hung up the phone.

There was no need for me to pack my bag and get on the bus to Mexico City. I did not have to get on that well-known, well-worn asphalt sprinkled with scattered garbage, lost gloves, used condoms, and old cigarette packs.

I did not have to take the highway my grandmother tried to cross carrying a jug of milk. I did not have to take the road that has always been a river of blood and white milk mixed with car oil.

I did not have to take the road that has killed at least twenty people since the day I was born as well as dogs, sheep, goats, horses, chickens, iguanas, and snakes.

I did not have to take the highway dotted with drops of blood from Maria's gunshot wound.

No.

I did not mention my mother's phone call to Julio or Jacaranda.

I felt as if my body were green inside like green logs that cannot burn in a fire. I felt too young to be out in the world.

I didn't even own a pair of shoes.

Three days later there was a knock at the front door.

Julio, Jacaranda, and I were in the kitchen having breakfast.

No one had ever knocked on the door. The person who was outside knocked again and then rang the doorbell. It was not really a ring as whoever had their finger on the small plastic ringer outside did not let up. The sound wailed through the house like a siren.

Julio stood and left the house and went out to the garden. Jacaranda and I walked over to the front door. It was wide open.

At the entrance stood three policemen. Their faces were covered with wool ski masks and they carried machine guns. They had come for me. They wanted to search the house.

Yes, come in, Jacaranda said.

The policemen made us walk with them as they checked all the rooms. When they inspected the master bedroom, they broke into the dressing room we had never been inside.

In the place where I had expected expensive dresses, beautiful blouses and sweaters, and sequined satin or velvet evening gowns was a large storage room. Instead of high-heeled satin shoes and fur coats, it contained hundreds of assault rifles, thousands of rounds of ammunition, cartridges of dynamite, grenades, and dozens of bullet-proof vests stacked in piles. There were even several guns, cradled like babies, in USA flags.

Julio and I had made love at the edge of carnage.

The first thing one of the policemen did in my small room was lift the mattress up off the bed.

My mother's words came to me across the hills and down the highway and straight into me, Only an idiot hides things under a mattress!

The policemen took the brick of heroin and Paula's notebook with the photos and told me to pack my bag.

Julio never said goodbye. He jumped over the garden fence as soon as he realized there were cops at the door. I'm sure he thought they were coming to get him. He, and his delicious rose and magnolia kisses, disappeared forever. He drowned in the river.

Do we shoot the grandma? one policeman asked.

I wonder if she's bulletproof? one of the other policemen answered and then he shot her.

Jacaranda fell backward on the marble.

Her body lay on the cold marble.

Blood from her head washed into her gray hair on the

white marble. Her eyes were open and fixed in a stare like the glass eyes of the stuffed animals from Africa.

One policeman handcuffed me and pushed me into a police car. We drove through the early-morning streets following the signs to the airport. From the car window, I could see the dirty streets and endless rows of T-shirt stores closed tight with metal curtains.

I saw a fisherman walking toward the beach with a pole resting over his shoulder and a small red plastic child's bucket in one hand.

I looked toward the Pacific Ocean to the place where I knew the Virgin Mary was drowning under the waves.

Mrs Domingo's diamond ring was still on my hand. I turned the diamond inward, toward my palm, so that it looked as if I were only wearing a gold wedding band.

I knew an army helicopter would take me to Mexico City. My crime was too important to be handled by the state of Guerrero. Thanks to television, I had done all this before. I knew exactly what was going to happen.

I knew I was going to go straight to the women's jail because I was a witness and an accomplice to the murder of a little girl who was the daughter of one of Mexico's most important drug traffickers. This was the crime that had captured the nation.

If I had not stopped watching television at the marble house, I would have known that the brutal killing of a girl shocked the world. I would have known that a teacher from a rural community claimed it was vultures that led him to the shack. He told one reporter that there were over twenty vultures above and they looked like a cloud of black feathers swimming in the air.

In the helicopter I sat with my back to the pilot. Only one policeman got in and sat straight in front of me. I had to lean forward on my seat since my hands were still handcuffed behind my back.

As we lifted off and rose above the port of Acapulco, the helicopter turned and headed toward Mexico City. I looked out the window and down on the jungle below. My feet began to feel cold in the plastic flip-flops as we reached a higher altitude.

There were two canisters stored between the two seats in front of me. They were labeled with the skull and crossbones symbol for poison. In large black letters I read the word *Paraquat.*

Eighteen

I didn't bother to look out the window when the helicopter flew over Mexico City. I'd always thought I'd visit the city's parks, museums, and the famous Chapultepec zoo and castle, but now I knew it would never happen.

The guard sitting across from me was still wearing the wool ski mask. The sweat from his scalp dripped down his neck and the front of his shirt. He was so sweaty that even his hand resting on the machine gun glistened. His eyes peered through the holes in the wool and looked into my eyes.

You're all a bunch of stupid girls, he said.

I looked away from him and out the window at the Popocatepetl volcano with the long plume of smoke blowing from its crater.

He shook his head back and forth.

All you stupid bitches care about is money.

My hands were handcuffed behind my back and I felt the diamond in my palm.

Long ago, my mother taught me how to protect myself against a man. She said to take my index finger and poke out the man's eyes, to just scoop them out like clams out of their shells. She did not teach me what to do if I were in handcuffs.

I never want to have a daughter, he said.

He took out a piece of gum and pushed it through the hole in the mask and into his mouth. His mouth moved under the wool, under the small round opening, as he chewed.

If I had a daughter, he said, I'd spit.

Nineteen

In Mexico City, before I was formally booked and taken to jail, I was paraded for the press in a room at the airport.

I was made to stand behind a long table that was covered with several dozen rifles, pistols, and ammunition. This was the cache of weapons that had been found at the house in Acapulco. The reporters screamed out questions at me and television cameras filmed my face.

Who killed her, you or Mike?

Why did you have to shoot her in the face like that?

Why? Why did you kill an innocent little girl?

What happened at that ranch?

Are you Mike's girlfriend?

As the reporters called out questions, I bowed my head, pressed my chin to my chest, and looked down toward my heart so they could not photograph my face. But then I remembered something. I looked up.

If I looked up, and let myself be filmed, my eyes would pierce right though the camera. In two seconds the image of my face would be beamed down into the bowl of the white satellite dish antenna my father had bought. In two seconds the image of my face would be beamed down straight into the television screen and right into my two-room home on our mountain. I knew that if I looked up into the cameras, I would see my mother as she sat in front of the TV with a beer in her hand and a yellow plastic flyswatter across her knee. I looked into the camera and deep into my mother's eyes and she looked back.

Part Three

Twenty

The Santa Marta Jail in the south of Mexico City was the biggest beauty parlor in the world. The bitter and citric scent of hair dyes, hair sprays, and nail polish permeated the rooms and passageways of the building.

The odors took me back to the day that Maria had her harelip fixed. It was the day a kettle of vultures circled above our home. And it was also the day my mother was angry with the Acapulco fortuneteller because the woman never predicted that my mother would have to bury someone.

Did that fortuneteller tell my mother that her daughter was going to go to jail?

In the prison office where I was booked there was a blackboard on the wall. A scrawl of white chalk kept track of the foreign inmates and children. In the jail there were seventy-seven children who were all under the age of six. There were three inmates from Colombia, three from Holland, six from Venezuela, three from France, one from Guatemala, one from the United Kingdom, two from Costa Rica, one from Argentina, and one from the United States.

After I was booked in and my photograph and fingerprints were taken, I was given a pair of clean beige sweatpants and a beige sweatshirt and told to change. The clothes were worn so thin I could see my skin beneath the weave. How many women had placed their arms in these sleeves before me?

The jail was a chessboard of beige and navy-blue squares. The women in beige were awaiting trial and the women in blue had been sentenced. In jail I learned that everyone would get hungry for yellow or green, as if colors had turned into food.

No one gave me a pair of shoes or sneakers.

I walked through the jail in my red plastic flip-flops with traces of Acapulco beach sand between my toes.

A female prison guard pushed me through the octagonal maze of corridors toward my cell. Instead of windows, long rectangular openings in the cement walls, like slashes from a knife, looked out on the main yard where a few women in navy blue kicked a ball around.

On the other side of the building, across the yard, was the men's prison. It was close enough to hear shrieks and cries coming from over the wall. The men and women prisoners could wave to each other from certain points.

My cell contained a bunk bed. When you are charged with killing the daughter of one of the country's most important drug traffickers you get special treatment. You get to share a cell with only one other prisoner. Most of the inmates had to share rooms with at least four people, two to a bed. I was placed in a cell with a foreigner because this makes it harder to be killed by orders from outside. I knew this. The person who killed that little girl had no chance of living, not for long.

The woman who shared my cell was also dressed in beige and was so small her sweatpants were rolled up around her ankles so she wouldn't trip. Her hair was pulled into a long black braid down her back and, when she turned towards me, I could see her left sleeve hung loose and empty, falling from her shoulder as if it were a flag on a day without wind.

Since the moment I had been taken from the house in Acapulco and brought to the jail, I could not hear my mother's voice. It had almost been forty-eight hours of silence. I heard the rush of my own blood through my body and it was the sound of Acapulco's ocean.

When I looked at the tiny, childlike woman, my mother's voice came back. Her words crossed the jungle, soared above the pineapple and palm trees, traveled over the mountains of the Sierra Madre, past the Popocatepetl volcano, down into the valley of Mexico City, and moved through the treeless streets straight into me.

So what the hell happened to your arm? I heard her ask.

Chop, chop, chop, the woman answered.

In a few moments I figured out that everything the woman said was plunk plunk this and splash splash that and clonk clonk, quack quack, bang bang.

I could hear my mother again. Right inside of my head she said, Well, well, well, look who's here! It's Miss Onomatopoeia herself!

Miss Onomatopoeia's name was Luna and she was from Guatemala. She pointed up at the top bunk with the pointer finger of her right hand, her only hand, and told me the top bunk bed was for me. She had long and square fake acrylic fingernails pasted onto her real nails and each nail was painted black and white in a zebra pattern.

One woman from El Salvador was up there, but she left yesterday. I hope it's clean, Luna said.

I am sure it's fine.

Nothing in here is fine. All that woman ever said was God. She said God all day long as if the word were her heart beating.

A woman dressed in blue appeared and stood within the door frame. She was so large she blocked out much of the light from the corridor. She had short black hair and long fingernails that were painted yellow. She'd been sentenced. If you wore blue, you had no hope. If you wore beige you had hope.

So you killed the baby, she said. It was you.

I shook my head.

Touch the floor.

I paused for a second and she said it again, Touch the floor!

I crouched and touched the ground with my fingers.

You're in jail, she said. I tell everyone who comes here to touch the ground as soon as they get here so they know exactly where they are. Now you have to decide if you left your pussy outside or if you brought it in here with you!

The woman moved to one side and the light from behind her body filled my cell. She smelled like blood and ink. She smelled like red and black. I was still crouched, touching the floor when she left.

Violeta, that's Violeta. She's killed two, no, three, no, four, no, many men. Bang bang, but with a knife, slice, slice, stab, stab.

How many men?

Many. She tattoos everyone and loves jail because there's so much skin in here.

The sunlight that fell through the narrow slat of the room's window was cold.

I never knew the sun could be cold.

Luna explained there was no place to keep anything but that I could store my belongings in a space under her bottom bunk bed.

I have no belongings.

You will in time.

No. This is a mistake.

Did you kill her? You did, right?

I looked into Luna's black eyes.

She was a small, dark brown Mayan Indian from Guatemala with straight black hair. I was a medium-sized, dark brown mix of Spanish and Aztec blood from Guerrero, Mexico, with frizzy, curly hair, which proved I also had some African slave blood. We were just two pages from the continent's history books. You could tear us out and roll us into a ball and throw us in the trash.

What do you think? I asked.

What?

Think I killed that girl?

Of course not, she answered. They say here that it was an AK-47. You can't know how to use one of those.

My mother's voice echoed through me. I heard her say, This Guatemalan Indian is a piece of candy.

Luna said I could borrow any of her things except her toothbrush.

Even though it was only midday, I climbed up into the bed and lay down. The beauty parlor smell of the prison was concentrated up there. It smelled like acetone nail polish remover mixed with lemon hair spray. The unpainted concrete ceiling was a foot away from my face. If I turned over and lay on my side, I could scrape my shoulder and hip against the rough cement.

In jail everyone is missing something, Luna said.

I curled up and tried to forget I was cold. I didn't have a blanket. If I wanted a blanket or pillow I had to buy it. Everything in jail had to be bought.

There was some graffiti written in black ink on the wall, exactly at my eye level and at the eye level of hundreds of women who had lain in the top bunk bed before me. Most of the graffiti consisted of lovers' hearts with initials in them. Also carved into the cement was the word *Tarzan*.

I closed my eyes. I could hear my mother say, So you had to go to jail and share a room with a one-armed Indian woman from Guatemala!

I also knew that even though we were proud to be the angriest and meanest people in Mexico, my mother could not stop crying because her daughter was in jail. The flies were drinking her tears.

When I thought of my house, I also knew that the drug trafficker's blue plastic asthma inhaler was still lying in the green grass under the papaya tree. I knew it would lie there for hundreds of years.

I slept for the rest of the day and all through the night. The dawn light awoke me along with the new sound of traffic. It was the first time I had risen without hearing birds. It was raining outside, which made the cement walls and floor seem like walls and floors of ice.

During the night Luna had covered me with a blanket and a couple of towels. Small acts of kindness could turn me inside out. I never would have believed that someone who had shot a child in a break-and-entry robbery, killed twelve old ladies for their wedding rings, or murdered two husbands could loan me a sweater, give me a cookie, or hold my hand.

Luna had also placed my feet inside plastic supermarket bags so they would not get cold in the night.

Julio had said, Life is a crazy place where the drowned can be walking on dry land.

Now I knew he was right. It only took me one day to figure out that being in jail was like wearing a dress inside out, a misbuttoned sweater, or a shoe on the wrong foot. My skin was on the inside and all my veins and bones were on the outside. I thought, I better not bump into anyone.

Twenty-One

I was tied to a train, the migrant train that goes from the south of Mexico to the US border, tied with a blue plastic clothesline, Luna said.

I could see her blood move through her veins and down her left arm and stop at the small stump, which was all that remained of her arm, like a tree limb that has been badly pruned with a dull saw.

I knew what Luna was talking about because Julio had told me that in Mexico there were two borders that cut the country into pieces. The horizontal border is the one between the United States and Mexico. The vertical border leads from Central America, through Mexico, and to the United States. Mostly men take the train from Central America to the border. It's much cheaper. Women prefer taking the bus because it is safer. Julio, like everyone else, called the train The Beast.

You took The Beast?

We tied ourselves to the train because you fall asleep, Luna explained. You can't help it. Imagine falling asleep in that speed. I was tied outside to a handrail. I went to sleep and slipped and fell beside the track and the train tore off my arm and I lost my arm and I almost died.

She said all of this and did not take a breath.

Luna said she liked being in jail because she could urinate whenever she needed to.

You don't want to get off to urinate when the train stops for a few minutes and the men get off because they'll watch you, make fun of you as you squat by the tracks, or rape you. All the women, all of us hold it in. It hurts. You don't want to drink and if you don't drink, well, you know, you die.

Did you leave Guatemala by yourself?

The train tore off my arm and I almost died and they still wanted to deport me. The migration police didn't believe me when I said I was Mexican. They told me to sing the Mexican national anthem if I was a Mexican.

Do you know it?

Luna shook her head.

This reminded me of the day I sat under a papaya tree with Paula and Maria going over the words of the national anthem. Paula and I learned it all so easily as if it was senseless sounds, but Maria took the actual words very seriously. What does that mean, exactly? she said. Why are we singing about Mexico going to war? Why does the inside of the world tremble?

I didn't kill that girl. I could never do that. I was in the car, locked in a car.

Luna unrolled a piece of toilet paper and handed it to me so I could blow my nose.

I'm not crying, I said.

Yes, you are.

No, I'm not.

Luna explained that, even though my mother was supposed to be notified, as I gave the administrators who booked me in her number, they probably would not call her.

They're slow, slow, slow about everything here if you don't have money. Money is a car race. Money is speed.

I could feel Mrs Domingo's diamond on the inside of my palm, closed in my fist.

You must borrow a person's telephone, Luna said. You have to call your mother or someone. Is there someone else?

No, there's no one else.

Are you married? Luna looked at the gold band on my finger.

No.

Georgia will let you make a call. She's the only one who might lend you her phone without making you pay.

Does everyone know that I'm here because they think I killed that girl?

Yes.

Someone is going to kill me, right?

Luna did not answer. She turned and left the cell.

I thought, If Mike's alive, he's dead.

In the small cell the bunk beds took up most of the room. Inside the cave-like space of Luna's bed, she'd hammered nails into the wall. On these nails she'd hung at least ten sleeves that she'd cut off of sweaters, blouses, and long-sleeved T-shirts. They were all beige and looked like a wall covered in snakes.

After only a few minutes, Luna returned and stood beside me as I looked at the sleeves hooked on the wall.

I did not take my arm into consideration, she said. I didn't give it a special place in my life. I am saving these sleeves because I am going to make an altar to my arm.

That's a good idea.

Do you give your arms a special place in your life?

No. No, I have not.

Listen. Stick to me. Don't go walking around alone.

Do you believe me, Luna?

Yes, maybe, maybe I believe you. Maybe.

There was a knock on the door. A woman was standing there dressed in navy-blue sweatpants. She had a canister on her back and was holding a long, thin metal hose in her hand.

No, no, Luna said. She stood up and held her one hand up in the air.

Do you want bedbugs and fleas? the woman asked in a whisper.

The old, dented tin fumigation canister was corroded at its seams and a dark yellow paste, like mucus, formed around the spout.

Shit, Luna said. Let's get out of here. She's going to fumigate. Do what you have to do, Aurora.

Aurora was as pale as one of those centipedes or worms one finds under rocks. They are pale because the creatures have never been in the sun. As a child I used to pry rocks out of the ground or kick them over in search of white or transparent insects. Aurora's light brown hair was so thin her ears stuck out from her hair.

This is Ladydi, Luna said.

I know, Aurora said in her drafty voice. Get out or stay in. It's up to you.

She pursed her lips tightly together so that the fumigation fumes would not get in her mouth. The tips of her ten fingers were deep yellow.

Do you have any aspirin? Aurora asked.

Luna didn't answer and I followed her out of the room. Behind us we heard the whooshing sound of the spray as insecticide filled our cell.

The truth is who wants fleas and bedbugs? Luna said.

You look pretty clean, but it's for the best. We won't be able to go in there for a while. That stink stays around and gives you a headache you can't shake off for days. You must be hungry by now. Let's get some food.

The rain had stopped but the sky was still cloudy.

I followed Luna down the labyrinth of corridors that all seemed the same. The men's prison could be seen through the long open glassless windows in the concrete walls. The faces of men at the windows looked in our direction. Every now and then one of them cupped his hands around his mouth and screamed something or lifted up a white T-shirt and waved it madly at us. It was as if the women's prison was a ship passing by and the men's prison was a deserted island with hundreds of shipwrecked sailors. In one short morning, I learned that the men do this non-stop, all day long, and if a woman waves back, it's love forever after.

And, unlike the male prison across the patio, this world overflowed with rubbish bins filled with bloodied cotton and rags. In this women's world blood was exposed in the garbage, in the unflushed toilet bowl, on sheets and blankets, and on the stained panties soaking in the corner of a sink. I wondered how much blood left this place in a day and coursed through the underground sewage system of Mexico City. I knew I was standing on a lake of blood.

Luna took me to a large room with long tables and benches. Prisoners sat around occupied with different activities. Some were eating, others were knitting, and some women breastfed their babies. Two boys, who were about four or five years old, played on the floor with a train set that was made of small cereal boxes attached with knitting wool. One long table was laid out with dozens of bottles of nail polish and nail polish remover. At least twenty inmates were sitting around painting their fingernails.

Painted on the back wall of the room was a mural framed by a banner that said *The Mural of Hearts.* The content of the work, which I later found out had been painted by the inmates over a span of several years, consisted of portraits of famous Mexican women. I looked at their faces and read the names: Sor Juana, Emma Godoy, Elena Garro, Frida Kahlo, and Josefa Ortiz de Dominguez.

As breakfast was no longer being served, Luna bought us each a sandwich from one of the prisoners. In jail everyone had a business and everything had a price, even toilet paper or Kotex.

Luna said she had no income but received help from a Guatemalan family in Mexico who were part of an evangelical organization that tried to convert prisoners.

They're all trying to convert us, Luna said. Mormons, Evangelists, Baptists, Methodists, Catholics. Everyone. The missionaries come to the jail on Sunday, and sometimes they get in on other days, you'll see. Every God is in this prison.

Luna suggested we go out and eat our sandwiches in the yard.

We can get some coffee there and watch the football and then see if we can talk to Georgia who has the telephone, she said.

To one side of the yard, twenty or so women were playing football. The other prisoners sat around on benches. When I looked up I could see a colony of faces. Dozens of women peered out from the windows. When I looked up to the opposite side, I could see the men's jail and their faces were also looking out of windows. Looking out of windows here was an activity. It was a way to live.

Those men, Luna said, pointing in the direction of the men's prison, they're looking for wives. Do you have a husband?

No.

If you get married he can come and visit you. They give you a room with a bed and everything.

No. I'm not married.

None of those men over there at the jail want to marry me, Luna said. Because of my arm. I really don't want a man, I want a baby. I want someone to love.

Even if they take the child away from you?

In jail a woman could only keep her child until the age of six.

It's six years of love at least, Luna said. And then you can have another. Do you want a baby?

Yes.

That's Georgia, Luna said, pointing to one of the women playing football.

Georgia was a tall, slim woman who looked thirty years old. She had blond hair and blue eyes. In the prison yard, she stood out among all the dark skin and hair. She looked like a stick of butter on a table.

She's from England, Luna explained. A woman from the British Embassy comes and visits her and gives her money, and her family sends money too.

Why is she here? What did she do?

She was coming to Mexico for a fashion show, Luna said. She worked in fashion. She had shoes.

Shoes?

Yes, two suitcases filled with them, the platform shoes, you know, the shoes with the big platforms?

Yes.

Those platform shoes were filled with heroin.

Heroin! Heroin! You've got to be kidding! What idiot brings heroin into Mexico?

That's what everyone says.

I thought of the hills and valleys around my house planted with red and white poppies. I thought of the towns on our mountain like Kilometer Thirty, or Eden. These were the towns along the old road to Acapulco and not the new highway that tore our lives in two pieces. These were the towns that you could only enter by invitation. If you accidently went there no one would ask you your name or ask you what time it was, they'd just kill you. Mike once told me that there were huge mansions in those towns and incredible laboratories that were built underground to turn the poppies into heroin. He said that a miracle occurred at Kilometer Thirty a few years ago. The Virgin Mary appeared in a piece of marble.

Passenger buses always went on this road in convoy. They were scared that they'd be stopped and robbed. This was the highway where decapitated bodies were hung from bridges. This was the highway where the bus drivers swore that at night they'd seen the ghosts. They had seen the ghost face of a clown or the vaporous image of two little girls holding hands as they walked down the side of the road.

No one on this highway stopped to buy tamarind candy or live turtles or starfish with five rays wriggling and squirming in the dry air.

There is an American girl living in the town of Eden. Now that is a backward story, Mike told me. Who comes here?

He said that one of Mexico's most important drug lords brought her back and she's only about fourteen years old. She's the man's third wife and she likes to take care of everyone's babies. She keeps to herself, Mike said. She likes to bake cakes.

The young American girl became a legend inside of me. I imagined her walking along our roads, drinking our water and standing under our sun.

Mike told me that at Christmas the drug lord brought in fake snow and covered the town with mountains of the white powder to make the American girl happy. He also ordered the building of a huge Christmas tree, which was made out of dozens of pine trees that were delivered from a pine-tree nursery near Mexico City. The drug trafficker placed the tall tree in the middle of the main square and had it covered with Christmas decorations.

But that was not the best thing he did, Mike said. The best thing he did was to bring reindeer to the town. He flew them in on one of his private airplanes from a ranch in Tamaulipas.

Have you seen this? I asked.

Yes. Imagine, he turns a piece of Guerrero into the North Pole.

Surrounded by cement, far from the ocean and seabirds and my mother, I thought, How the hell did Mike know all of this?

My hand ached to slap him across the face.

I listened to his stories and never really listened. Now I knew why he had all this information and why I was in jail accused of killing a drug lord, the drug lord's daughter, and having a package of heroin, worth a million and a half dollars, in my possession.

Where are you, Mike?

I thought, I am going to pray for you, Mike. I'm going to pray you remember me. I'm that deep line, from pinkie to thumb, in the palm of your right hand, Mike. The lifeline that gets full of dirt when you forget to wash.

In my mind I was talking to Mike, but in my eyes I was watching two dozen women playing football. One had *Chicharito* tattooed on her arm. Another woman had the full body image of the Virgin of Guadalupe on the outside of her right thigh.

They play football every day, Luna said. Even if it's raining they have tournaments. The three teams are Rainbow, Liberty and Barcelona.

The women ran and called out to each other. From here I could see Violeta who played with a lit cigarette in her mouth. She ran back and forth and never stopped puffing. The smoking butt sat in her mouth as she moved. When she approached a scuffle for the ball, she would throw her head backward, in a gesture that reminded me of a bird drinking water. She did this so that she would not burn anyone with the fiery tip of her cigarette. Her extremely long fingernails that were painted yellow yesterday now were green. From where I sat, only a few feet away, her fingernails looked like long parrot feathers coming out of the tips of her fingers.

Violeta is the captain, Luna said.

As we watched the game Aurora, who had finished fumigating our room, slunk toward us. She was still carrying the canister on her back. She sat down beside us.

You can go to your room now, Aurora said.

I squirmed a little from her odor. I had noticed her yellow fingertips but, outside in the daylight, I realized her skin and the whites of her eyes were also jaundiced.

No, we're not going in for a while, Luna said.

Do you have any aspirin? Aurora asked.

Don't tell me you've finished all yours again? You'll get a hole in your stomach!

My head hurts.

Aurora lay down. She curled up on her side on the ground on the cold and damp cement. It seemed like the coldest piece of the planet on that cloudy morning. I wanted to touch her and caress her head as if she were a stray dog in the street. But, as with a stray dog, I was afraid to touch her because she might give me a disease. As she lay beside me, I even thought I could see mange on the side of her head, under her stringy hair.

If my mother were there she would have said, She deserves to be run over by a car!

The football game ended and Luna called out to Georgia to come over. Georgia walked slowly while Violeta followed behind, still puffing on a cigarette. When they reached us Violeta squatted down on her heels in front of me so that we were eye-to-eye. She rested her hands on her knees so that her nails were stretched out before her. Close up her nails no longer made me think of feathers. Instead, they were like the talons of hawks and vultures that swarmed above my house back in the jungle. Violeta's nails looked like they could pick up a rabbit or a mouse and carry it off. The nails could tear at flesh. They could scratch someone's face to pieces.

So this is Ladydi? Georgia said. She looked at me. Her blue eyes and my black eyes met. I knew she was thinking, So, this is the dark and ugly creature who has my beautiful princess's name!

I wanted to say, I'm sorry, but I had never said I'm sorry to anyone.

I thought of all the Ladydi dolls I had at home. To this day, the Lady Diana dolls my father brought me back from the United States were still in my room in their original cardboard and plastic boxes so the jungle mould would not destroy them. I had a Lady Diana doll in her wedding dress, a Lady Diana in the gown she wore to meet President Clinton, and a Lady Diana doll in riding clothes. My father had even given me a plastic jewelry set of Lady Diana's pearls. These I wore until they broke. The white plastic pearls were kept in a cup in the kitchen.

I felt like counterfeit money, fake designer clothing at the Acapulco market, like a Virgin of Guadalupe made in China. I looked at Georgia and turned into cheap plastic. My mother had given me the biggest fake name she could find. How could I begin to explain to this British woman that my name was an act of revenge and not an act of admiration? How could I explain that my name was payment for my father's infidelities?

Close up, Georgia was so pale I could see the blue veins under her skin. Her face was covered in freckles, even on her lips and eyelids. Her eyelashes and eyebrows were colorless and so her eyes were unframed and looked like two sky-blue marbles resting on her cheeks.

I hear you want my phone, she said.

Yes. Please.

I'm not going to charge you this time because we're both British, right? And, after all, you're a princess.

Violeta and Luna laughed at this. Aurora didn't seem to listen. She was still curled up like a white-yellow centipede beside me. I could smell the insecticide rise from her body in small gusts every time she took a breath.

Georgia reached under her sweatshirt. She took out a phone from under her clothing that was hidden in a seam. It was cloaked in a Cadbury's chocolate bar wrapper. She gave me the phone and I could see her hands were also covered with freckles.

Good luck, Princess, she said.

And then she curtsied.

Georgia was liked because she was a foreigner and had money. But no one respected her stupid crime. Everyone in jail made fun of her and gave her shoes as presents on her birthday and at Christmas. There was always someone who would tease her and yell things like, Hey, Blondie, why don't you bring some tacos or some guacamole to Mexico too?

Those of us who had killed were different. It was not exactly respect that we were given. It was like the respect for a rabid dog. People circled around us. Here no one wanted the killers to cook or handle food. The prisoners were superstitious about eating food touched by a killer's hand.

Georgia and Violeta turned and walked away. Aurora stirred on the ground beside me.

I'm hungry and thirsty, Aurora said. Does anyone have any gum?

Aurora was just like Maria. Maria used to think that gum was a substitute for water and food. This unexpected memory of Maria made me want to cover my eyes with my hands and disappear from the prison into the dark skin of my palms. The last time I saw Maria, my half-sister, my sweet friend with her harelip curse, had been when they'd wheeled her into a cubicle in the emergency room at the Acapulco clinic with a bullet in her arm.

We'd better go back to our cell so you can make that call, Luna said. You don't want to get caught, and they'll catch you anywhere else.

We stood up and walked toward the building. Aurora stayed behind and continued to lie curled up on the cement ground.

Georgia teases everyone, Luna said. Don't feel bad

about that. She doesn't give a shit about my arm. She's always throwing things at me and yelling at me to catch. Sometimes she calls me Catch. That's my nickname.

As we walked in the blue-and-beige chessboard world, my eyes longed for green plants, yellow and red parrots, blue ocean and sky. The colorless color of cement made me feel hot and cold at the same time. So, when I sat in my cell, which still smelled of insecticide, I didn't only call my mother. I called the leaves, palm trees, red ants, jade-green lizards, yellow-and-black pineapples, pink azaleas, and lemon trees. I closed my eyes and prayed for a glass of water.

Luna sat beside me. She sat so close I felt her ribcage against me where she should have had an arm. Her face was full of anticipation and hope.

Oh, let's pray someone answers, she said.

Luna pressed so close to me I felt she wanted to slip on my flip-flops, get in my worn jail uniform and into my skin. It was as if she were calling her own mother.

Of course my mother had been standing at the clearing all day and all night. She held her telephone up in the air until she felt the tired ache and burn of her muscles down from her fingers to her waist. I knew she'd been standing there pacing and pacing. No one was there. Everyone had left the mountain and she stood there alone and thought about how our world fell apart. Paula was stolen and then she and her mother left forever. Ruth was stolen. Augusta had died from AIDS and Estefani was living in Mexico City with her grandmother and siblings. I wondered where Maria and her mother were, but I knew they'd left our piece of land and sky. After everything Mike had done they must have looked for a place to hide. In the state of Guerrero no one wonders if someone is going to come and get you, you know they *will* get you, so you don't stick around.

My mother was the last living soul on our mountain. She stood alone with the ants and scorpions and vultures.

The phone rang and she answered.

Thank God I have been a robber all of my life, Ladydi!

It was the first thing she said.

Thank God I have been a robber all of my life, Ladydi!

It was the second thing she said.

I'm going to sell everything. Thank God I've been a thief all my life now I can sell it all. Ladydi, listen to this. I have five gold chains, several pairs of earrings and six silver teaspoons buried in a can of milk at the back of the house. No one would think of looking there! Isn't that just perfect? Tell me where you are, sweet sugar baby. I'll be there in two days. Goodbye.

My mother hung up her phone. She had not even waited for me to tell her where I was.

So, is she coming? Luna asked.

Yes. In two days.

My mother would never come for me, Luna said. She's in Guatemala. She doesn't even know I'm here. She doesn't even know her little girl has lost an arm. Of course she won't care.

She won't care about your arm?

You don't know her.

You're her daughter.

When she sees me she's going to ask me where I left my arm as if I'd left a sweater or a hat behind and need to go back and get it. She isn't going to want me around with one arm. She's going to say I can't work in the field and that no man will ever want to look at me.

She has to understand.

My mother is going to say, What can you carry?

Oh, really?

I never buried my arm, Luna said. Does one bury parts of oneself?

I don't know.

I don't know. I don't know where it is or what happened to my arm.

Why did you leave Guatemala?

Because I wanted to have dollars. I hated my life in Guatemala, Luna said.

It was bad?

My husband beat me every day. No. He did not beat me. He slapped me across the face. That's what he did. Slap, slap, slap. All day long. My cheek became a part of his hand.

So you came alone?

Yes, Luna answered. I thought anything was better than that, but I was wrong.

Yes, you were wrong.

All kinds of people are trying to go north, she said. You cannot imagine the things people take across the border to the United States. I saw stacks of dried-out stingrays that looked like sheets of black leather. I saw boxes filled with orchids. The police X-ray the trucks and buses. The X-rays find the white skeletons of immigrants. They see the human bones twisted with rickets and they find pumas and eagles, they see the bird skeletons. One man had two baby toucans in his jacket pocket.

Yes, I said. In Acapulco people steal turtle eggs.

Luna said we had to hurry and give Georgia back her phone. She'll never lend it again if we don't quickly give it back. She's counting the minutes.

We left our cell and went back to the large room where the inmates gathered together. It was late afternoon and some of the prisoners were taking workshops. Classes were offered in collage, painting, computers, reading and writing.

In the room every other inmate was having her hair done. Two women were sitting in front of a small mirror gluing false eyelashes onto their upper eyelids.

Georgia was sitting at a table with Violeta. I handed her the phone hidden in the chocolate-bar wrapping and thanked her.

No problem, Princess, she said. You're my princess so you can have it anytime.

Yes, thank you.

She's getting her birth certificate here, right? Georgia asked Luna. You told her?

Yes, Luna said.

How old are you?

I'm sixteen.

You know you don't have to be here, right? The law says you're still a child, Princess.

My mother will be bringing my birth certificate. She knows.

You have to get out before you're eighteen or you'll never get out. Isn't this true?

Violeta nodded her head. That's what happened to me. I came in at seventeen, but I was sentenced to thirty years when I was eighteen!

Make sure you get out before you're eighteen! When's your birthday?

Not until November.

So you have plenty of time, Georgia said. But hurry up. Hurry! I'm telling you this because you're my princess.

Violeta coughed. Her hands were on her hips and her long fingernails curled toward her stomach.

If you stay here you have to imagine that there is nothing else but this. Nothing else exists but this jail and the women in it. If you think that there is anything else, you won't survive, Violeta said in a hoarse smoker's voice.

Damn, you don't need to tell her that! What are you trying to do, break her heart? Georgia said.

Yes. Yes. She needs a broken heart, Violeta said.

That night there was nothing to do in the cell but lie in bed and talk to Luna. Some women had radios in their rooms, but Luna had nothing. There was no light, as she didn't have money to buy a light bulb for the fixture in the ceiling. She bought toilet paper by the square.

I lay in my bunk bed in the dark above Luna on my cement bed, which had no mattress. The room still smelled acrid from the fumigation. Luna's sweet voice came to me from thc bunk below.

When I look at Georgia I remember my mother once told me that rain falling while the sun is shining causes freckles, she said.

That's what makes a rainbow.

Yes, but also freckles.

Why is Violeta in here?

She's killed many men but she's in here because she killed her father. She does not regret it. She will tell you this over and over again. She has no regrets. She's happy to be here. Her father killed her mother. Violeta did it for her mother and everyone agrees she did the right thing.

Has she been in here a long time?

Yes. Her father never hugged her but when she killed him, as he died, he held on to her. She says she had to kill him for him to hug her.

She doesn't seem to like me.

She loves Georgia. She even made a collage for her as a present.

Luna explained that some of the inmates liked to take the collage workshop. It was given by a man, an artist, who had been teaching at the jail for years.

We cut out things from magazines, glue them on cardboard, and tell the stories of our lives. Will you come too? she asked.

Yes. Of course.

When you make a collage, you can really admire yourself.

I could hear Luna swallow and turn in the bunk beneath mine.

And what about Aurora? I asked. Why is she here?

Aurora. Aurora. Aurora. Luna said her name like a sigh.

Why is she here?

Aurora put the rat poison in the coffee.

Twenty-Two

The next morning when I opened my eyes the first thing I saw was the word *Tarzan* carved into the wall. It was as if the wall was tattooed to remind me where I was not. There were no birds, or plants, or the scent of overripe fruit.

Luna was already up and I heard her moving around. She sounded like a squirrel beneath me. I could hear her rummaging through plastic bags or dumping them out and scratching through them.

Damn, someone stole it, she said. Damn. Damn.

I didn't have the energy to ask what she was missing. I lay in silence. I heard a baby crying down the hall and I thought of the list on the blackboard in the administration office. There were seventy-seven children in this jail and in the morning they made a lot of noise.

Yesterday, when we had walked around the jail, Luna had taken me past two small rooms that were the children's school. Children could be in jail with their mothers until the age of six. The women got pregnant during their conjugal visits, which the jail allowed. Some of them also got pregnant because they were hired out as prostitutes by the guards at the criminal courts and tribunals. These encounters took place in the bathrooms.

Inside the jail's makeshift school a poster of a tree was pinned to the wall. If you are born and have grown up in jail, you have never seen a tree. There were also flashcards taped to a board that showed images of a bus, a flower, and a street. There was a flashcard of the moon.

Damn, Luna said again beneath me. Did you steal my lipstick?

I said, Jesus, Luna, who could want your jailbird lipstick with your jailbird saliva all over it?

The rustling below me stopped.

She did not know that it was my mother who had just spoken out of my mouth.

I climbed down from my bunk, sat on the edge of Luna's bed, and watched her make up her face.

When she'd finished, she placed her rouge and mascara in a plastic sandwich bag and pushed it under the bed. Then she turned and held my chin with her hand and looked at me.

You will see your mother soon and begin to get out of here. Get through these days, Ladydi. Don't fall down and scrape your knees yet, she said.

Why are you here? You have not told me. Will you get out soon?

Come to the collage workshop. It's fun. We all go.

Who?

Well, Aurora, Georgia, and Violeta, and a few others of course. Ladydi, let's go.

I slipped on my flip-flops and followed her down the corridor.

On the plastic worktables were stacks of magazines, pieces of cardboard, kindergarten scissors, and tubs of glue.

The teacher introduced himself and told me to look

through the magazines and cut out images that would then make up a story I wanted to tell. His name was Mr Roma. He had been giving these workshops at the jail for years. The reason many of the prisoners liked to take his class was that they make collages about their own lives but also because they were fascinated by Mr Roma. He was a painter. His hands were speckled with white oil paint. He had long, light brown curly hair that he tied into a ponytail. He was about fifty years old.

As Mr Roma showed me to a worktable and pulled out a stool for me, a few other women came in and sat at other worktables. They were all dressed in blue. Some shook the teacher's hand and others kissed him on the cheek.

Luna walked over to a cupboard where sheets of cardboard were stacked on shelves and took out her collage. She held the cardboard between her teeth and picked up a pair of scissors and glue. She sat beside me. She managed to get all her materials organized by using one hand and her front teeth.

There was a sudden quiet in the class as one prisoner walked past toward the sunless patio. I had not seen her before, but I knew she was jailed here. Everyone in Mexico knew about her. She was a celebrity. Four or five prisoners surrounded her, guarding her. Her frizzy black hair was combed upward so it looked like a crown. She was tall and wore navy blue, but I could see it was navy-blue velvet; it shimmered like a furry spider. Her wrists were covered with gold bangles and there was a gold ring on every one of her fingers, even on her thumbs. The prisoner was Lourdes Rivas. Her nickname was 'the nurse'. She was the wife of one of Mexico's top politicians. She was caught stealing millions of dollars from the Red Cross, which she had run for over twenty years.

Everyone in the class turned to look at her as she walked past.

I remembered hearing about her on the news. Someone had calculated that, thanks to her theft, thousands of ambulances were not purchased and hundreds of health clinics were not built. Her house was in San Diego, California, and was filmed for a television documentary about corruption in Mexico. My mother and I had watched it. We had even seen her bathroom sinks that were made of gold.

We watched her walk past with the small army of women prisoners that she paid to keep her safe. Everyone hated her. Everyone wanted to kill her. It seemed like every Mexican had a story about an ambulance that had never arrived.

On the table Luna's collage lay beside my empty piece of cardboard.

From the pages of *Vogue, People, National Geographic,* and soap-opera magazines Luna had cut out dozens of pictures of arms and had glued this collection all over her cardboard. In the middle of this mosaic of limbs, there were two infants with big blue eyes in diapers that looked as if they had been cut out from an infant formula advertisement. In the dimpled chests of both little girls, Luna had pasted red pieces of paper, cut in the shape of drops, falling from the bodies to a pool of cutout drops. They were like cutout Valentine's Day hearts.

You killed those children? I asked. I wanted to cover my mouth and take the words back into me, but it was too late. The words were there, in the air between us, and Luna swallowed them.

Yes. I killed them. It was snip, snip, snip. Children are so soft. The knife goes right in like cake.

She answered as if she were giving me a recipe.

Were they yours?

Oh, yes, of course, Luna answered. All mine. My two little girls.

Why?

They were always hungry, Luna answered. They always wanted to go to the swings in the park and I didn't have time for that. There are enough girls anyway. We really don't need any more.

Prisoners began to arrive for the classes. In other areas of the room knitting and computer classes were being held.

Georgia and Violeta appeared and sat down on the empty stools beside me. Georgia was dressed in a clean and new blue sweater. She was also wearing new tennis shoes and thick, fluffy white socks that were folded over at the ankle and covered the top of her sneakers. She placed a large red box of chocolates on the table and opened it.

Good morning, Princess, Georgia said. Have some English chocolate.

The chocolates looked like brown marbles. I took one and let it dissolve in my mouth. The creamy milk cocoa coated my teeth and tongue.

Georgia loved the collage workshop because of the fashion magazines. They reminded her of the catwalk world she used to belong to back in London before she and the Cobbler, as Violeta liked to call Georgia's boyfriend, filled up dozens of wedgies and pumps with heroin.

Violeta took the workshop very seriously. She lined up her glue and scissors with meticulous care. She had to move things around and organize her space with the pads of her thumbs because she did not want to break her long nails. Before she began, she lit up a cigarette and looked at her collage for the time it took to finish smoking the whole thing. By the end of the class she had smoked at least thirty cigarettes one after the other.

In her raspy voice she told me about her work. She told me the story of her life.

Here, she said, pointing to the far right of her collage, is the beginning of my life. See. Look. I was happy.

In this area of the cardboard Violeta had glued photographs of roses and two yellow-and-white-furred kittens playing with a ball of wool.

Then my mother and my father began to fight, Violeta said and pointed at a cutout photograph of Brad Pitt, which she had used to be the image of her father.

Don't leave out how he used to beat her, Georgia said.

He used to beat her badly, Violeta said and pointed to a photograph of an old lady from a cake-mix advertisement. The fighting went on for years and years.

Now comes the sad part, Georgia said. Get out your Kleenex.

Then I met a man, a bad man, Violet said. She pointed to the cutout image of the Marlboro man and his horse. He gave me drugs.

In the space on the collage between the Marlboro man and a cutout fire, which looked like the image of a gas explosion, Violeta had glued images of syringes and pill bottles. Under these drug images she used letters to spell out the word *prostitute.*

That's what I was, she said.

After the word she had cut out dozens of men's faces from shaving cream and shampoo ads. Among these unknown men's faces, I could make out the face of Pelé.

If you follow the sequence of my collage, Violeta

explained, you can see clearly that it was after the fire that I killed my father.

Good for you! Georgia said without looking away from her *Marie Claire* magazine.

Do you know that man there? I pointed to the face. That's a photo of Pelé, the greatest football player of all time.

Are you sure?

Of course I'm sure.

Georgia peered out of her magazine and looked down at the collage. Yes, that's him, she agreed. That's Pelé.

Oh well, Luna added from where she sat working on the cardboard land of her lost arm and dead children.

Just cover him up with another damn face. Who the fuck cares? Georgia said.

At this moment Aurora arrived like a stray cat that creeps in and rubs up against your leg. She slid onto a stool next to Violeta and folded her arms on the table and rested her head down.

Mr Roma stood at our table with his hands in his pockets and looked at Violeta's collage. It's almost finished, right? he said.

It's just missing one part.

Oh. What's that?

You know I'm honest, teacher. You know I'm a delinquent.

Everyone paused and looked up when Violeta said she was a delinquent. Georgia put down her magazine. Luna looked up from her collage where she was applying some fresh glue. Aurora did not move but opened her eyes and looked straight at Violeta.

You know I'm a delinquent, Violeta repeated. When I get out of here I only have one goal, one thing I am going to treat myself to. I want to eat you from head to foot. I want you in my bed, in my arms, smelling your rich, delicious essence, or, in other words, I want to have sex with you.

We looked from Violeta to Mr Roma to see what he would say.

Yes, Violeta, he said.

I'm serious. I'll be ringing your doorbell.

I know.

I guessed he'd heard it hundreds of times.

Mr Roma, Violeta said, you smell like a man, a real man.

Even though Luna had placed a blank piece of cardboard in front of me at the worktable, I could not work on a collage. I could not pick up one of those blunt scissors. Just looking at them made me feel as if I were back in kindergarten.

Instead, I looked through a *National Geographic* magazine. I opened the pages randomly and found an article on manatees. There were five images of manatees nursing their calves. The sea animals seemed to smile as they held their infants with their flippers.

I don't have to make a collage in order to talk about my life, Georgia said. I know that fucking tomcat is in a pub with who knows who, probably a wife, listening to Adele, while I'm here. I know he's eating a pork pie.

Violeta turned to Georgia and said, Just keep thinking about the Cobbler. Drive yourself crazy.

Maybe he even has kids by now. It's been three years and he's never answered one letter I've written to him, not one. What do you think of that, Princess? she asked me directly.

What can Ladydi know? Violeta said. Why on earth do you ask her?

He was my love. If I were to do a collage, I'd just glue all the letters to him that have been returned to me, Georgia said. The collage can be called *Return to Sender.*

Everyone was silent for a minute.

Violeta cupped her hand over Georgia's hand.

Aurora stirred beside her and stretched out her arms.

Don't be sad, Aurora said.

And this was when I saw the inside of her arm, lying across the table of scissors, glue, and magazines like a piece of pale, almost white, driftwood. Her skin was so wasted I could see the blue veins clearly as if they were sitting on her skin not in her skin.

There are symbols that don't need words like the cross, or the swastika, or the letter Z, or the skull and crossbones, which are on the label of any bottle of rat poison.

The symbol on the inside of Aurora's left arm was of a circle, with a dot in the middle, made with the burning tip of a cigarette: circle, polka dot, pink circle.

When I looked at that symbol I looked at Paula sitting under a tree, right on the ground, with insects crawling all over her body. Paula had unfolded her arm and laid it out before me to show the round cigarette burns on the inside skin.

Someone, a woman, someone, decided on this a long, long time ago and now we all do it, Paula had explained. If we're found dead someplace everyone will know we were stolen. It is our mark. Cigarette burns on the inside of your left arm are a message.

I reached across the worktable, my hand moved through the pots of glue, paintbrushes, and small stacks of magazines, and took hold of Aurora's arm. I grabbed her wrist and twisted it even more so that I could look at her branding more clearly. Her arm was a map.

Aurora raised her yellowed eyes and looked into mine. Her face was so sad that it occurred to me that she'd never smiled. The skin on her face had never been creased with joy.

In her asthmatic, breathless voice, damaged and hoarse from the fumigation fumes, she asked, Are you really Ladydi? Are you Paula's friend?

She spoke the words carefully as if she didn't want to break the words with her teeth.

It was this human centipede who told me the story of my life.

Everyone at the table listened as Aurora spoke in a wheezy voice like a breeze falling over us.

At the collage table, in the recreational room of a jail, Luna, Georgia, and Violeta learned about Paula, Estefani, and Maria. My life had suddenly turned into a wishbone. Aurora had brought both pieces together. She was the joint.

In that cement jail, Luna, Georgia, and Violeta saw my mountain and heard how my people gave birth to the most beautiful girl in Mexico. They learned about Maria's harelip operation and Ruth's hair salon and later disappearance. When Aurora told them that Ruth was a garbage baby this shocked a group of women criminals who could not be shocked.

My God! Luna exclaimed. Who would let their baby die all alone in a garbage heap?

Aurora told the story about how we used to blacken our faces and cut our hair so that we would not look attractive and how we would hide in holes if we heard drug traffickers approaching. Aurora described the day we came upon the poppy field and the downed army helicopter. Through gasps and gulps, she also told about the day that Paula was drenched with Paraquat and we had to wash her off with water scooped out of the toilet bowl. Aurora told them that Mike had a pet iguana tied with a string that followed him everywhere until his mother made iguana soup with it.

That was not nice, Georgia said.

Iguana soup is an aphrodisiac, Aurora said.

Who the fuck is Mike? Violeta asked.

Maria's brother, Aurora explained.

If I had been your mother, Georgia said to me, I would have run off that mountain as soon as Ruth disappeared. What was your mother waiting for?

No, Violeta said, I would have left as soon as your father went to the United States and had another family over there. He threw dirt at you. He buried you. I'm sure you have a bunch of English-speaking brothers and sisters living in New York.

Aurora said, No. No. No. Ladydi's mother would never leave that mountain because her dream and hope was that Ladydi's father would come back. That was her hope and, if she left their home, he would never find them.

I looked at Aurora and thought I was looking into a mirror. She knew my life better than I did.

And, let me tell you one thing more, Aurora said. Maria is Ladydi's half-sister.

Oh, please! Violeta said. Don't tell me that! Violeta threw down her short plastic glue brush and jumped up from her stool. Her long yellow nails flashed in the air like hornets. Oh, no, no, no. No! You're not going to tell me that your father fucked Maria's mother!

Georgia slapped her magazine down on the worktable. What a fucker!

Your poor mother, Luna said. She should have killed him. I would have killed him.

Georgia patted Luna's hand across the table. We know that, Luna, Georgia said. You don't have to tell us. Killing is your solution to everything.

Ladydi's mother never would have done that. That would have been like killing Frank Sinatra!

Paula had told our story to perfection.

Aurora gasped and wheezed. Talking this much had exhausted her. Holding her body up was an effort. She leaned down and rested her head on her arm. Her frail pulse quivered in her slender wrists and at her temples.

It was Violeta who stopped Aurora from talking. She said, That's enough, Aurora. You can finish the story tomorrow.

Violeta placed the glue brush in a jar of water. She stood and wrapped her clawed hand around the fumigation canister's strap and threw it over her shoulder. Then, holding her lit cigarette between her teeth, she picked up Aurora in her arms like a bride or a baby and carried her off. Violeta looked like a bird of prey with a rabbit in its claws. I wondered if those canisters, and Aurora herself for that matter, might be flammable so close to Violeta's burning cigarette.

Do you know how Violeta killed her father, Princess? Georgia asked me.

I shook my head.

You haven't told her, Catch? Georgia said.

She didn't ask.

In jail if you don't ask, Princess, no one tells.

Maybe she doesn't want to know, Luna said. Not everyone wants to know.

Oh, please! Everyone wants to know about murder! She placed her magazine on the pile in the middle of the table.

It's time to call Scotland, she said and walked off down the same corridor Violeta, with Aurora in her arms, had taken moments before.

Georgia called her father in Edinburgh every evening. She was her father's only child. Georgia hadn't seen her mother since she was a little girl. Her mother abandoned the family and ran off with a lover. Georgia's father had spent most of his money to help Georgia have everything she needed in jail. Her father had even mortgaged their small house to pay for Georgia's lawyers who were trying to get her extradited to the UK. Georgia swore she didn't know the shoes were filled with heroin but no one believed her.

What about that betrayal? Luna said.

Do you think it's true? I asked.

Of course it's true. Yes. I have a golden rule. I always believe a woman over a man.

Everyone in jail hated Georgia's boyfriend.

He better not show up at this jail, Luna said.

The truth was that only one man was adored in the jail and this was Georgia's father. He had become a legend. There was not a single daughter in that jail who was loved by their father, not one. Every prisoner was hoping that Georgia's father would scramble the money together to come to Mexico and visit. The women wanted to meet him and the ongoing project was to start a 'Bring Georgia's Father to Mexico' fund. Violeta had his name tattooed on her arm. It was blue on her limb and it went downward, like the down column in a crossword puzzle, and read *Tom.*

Georgia had new clothes, shoes, bedding, and bathroom articles because her father sent her packages and money every week. Her cell was filled with British sweets. Georgia shared her Cadbury bars and red boxes of Maltesers with everyone.

As Georgia walked away to call her father, a chill filled the room, and we heard thunder. Cool air blew through the corridors and glassless windows.

Mr Roma placed his materials away in the short metal locker at the back of the room. Luna stood and laid her collage, along with the other cardboard sheets, on a table in the back. I stacked the magazines in a pile.

The teacher said goodbye to Luna and, when he said goodbye to me, he kissed my cheek. Welcome to the workshop, he said. I hope you'll come back.

He smelled like beer.

I didn't rub his kiss away with my sleeve.

As Luna and I walked slowly back to our cell, the wet male saliva dried on my cheek. I felt the place on my face for hours afterward as if his kiss had left a mark on me. To have a man kiss you in a women's jail is a gift better than any birthday or Christmas present. It's better than a bouquet of roses. It's better than a warm shower. I could imagine living in this jail for years and living for every workshop day and that male kiss on my cheek. That kiss was rain, sunshine, and the sweet air of outside. Yes. I knew I'd even sit there and glue stupid things onto cardboard sheets just to get that kiss again.

Later that night, as I lay above Luna in our cement bunk beds, she chattered at me in the dark. The first night I thought she was just being nice and talking to me, but now I realized she had to talk to fill the darkness. Her chatter soothed and made me drowsy.

Luna said, Can you believe that there are only twenty-six letters to say everything? There are only twenty-six letters to talk about love and jealousy and God.

Yes.

Have you realized that the words of the day are not the same as the words of the night? Luna asked.

Yes.

In the dark I could hear large trucks and buses drive by the jail. The outside sounds could only be heard early in the morning and late at night.

If you've been here for two years, why haven't you been sentenced or extradited? I asked.

Princess, I never called a lawyer, or the Guatemalan Embassy or my family. I think everyone has forgotten that I'm here.

I'm sure they miss you.

No. You might ask how can the world forget about a human being, but it happens all the time.

But don't the people here in the jail wonder?

They assume I'm working on it. No one can imagine that I'd rather be here than anywhere else, but it's true.

You want to stay here?

Some like it better inside than outside, Luna said. This is the best place I've ever been. In my village the government massacred everyone.

In Guatemala?

I lost most of my family in just two years. I walked around thinking a cold bullet was going to pierce my body at any moment. A cold bullet.

The wind that had begun as a breeze during the collage workshop was now strong and the cold air entered the building in great gusts.

I thought going to the United States would be better. I heard all the stories, Luna said.

Some say there's nothing worse.

I've heard people get so thirsty they cut their arms and

suck out some blood. This is in the desert. Arizona. I've seen cuts on a man who tried to cross but was sent back. A border guard shoots you like a wolf, if you're lucky. If a cartel kidnaps you, like the Zetas, then you go to the land of dead immigrants, a special death place, without a birth certificate or gravestone, and nothing is worse than this. When Luna mentioned the border guard I could only think about Julio. The prayer that could bring him back to my life did not exist.

The first big drops of rain fell on the roof and the air smelled like a mixture of water and cement.

My father's in the United States, I said.

Imagine that a gun shooting at you is the last thing you see when you die. Imagine that being the very last image of life that you take to heaven. Do you think that the last thing you see matters?

My father is in New York, I said.

Listen, no way do I want to be buried in a cemetery with all those dead people. I want to be cremated. Do you?

I feel cold.

Yes, it's cold.

I'll need some blankets soon or I'm going to get sick.

You can come down here and sleep with me, Luna offered. I don't mind.

I sat up and scrambled down the side of the bunk bed. Luna lifted up the covers for me.

Get in, she said.

We curled up together and her body warmth entered my skin.

There, there, she said and hugged me with her arm. I felt the ghost limb of her missing arm surround me. Luna used her teeth to clench the top of the covers and pull them up to our chins.

I had known the mercy of scorpions. Now I knew the mercy of a killer.

Twenty-Three

Aurora's cell smelled like the fumigation poison. It was a larger cell than mine as it had two bunk beds and four women lived in the room. It also had a toilet, sink, and small shower all lined up in a row at the back of the cell.

Aurora received no help from the outside. She had to take the jobs that no one wanted. She had been the jail fumigator ever since she'd been sentenced over a year ago.

There was no one in the room but Aurora. She was lying down on one of the bottom bunks. She beckoned for me to come in.

I sat on the edge of her bed while she lay under the covers. On her bed, pushed up against the wall, were dozens of plastic supermarket bags and two fumigation canisters and their hoses. Aurora's eyes followed my gaze.

There's no storage space in this room, she said. We all have to keep our belongings on our beds.

Aurora's plastic bags were filled with clothes and objects that prisoners had given to her. In jail there was a superstition that if you took your belongings with you, you would come back. Aurora was a pack rat and accepted everything.

When you leave here, don't forget to give me your things, she said.

I don't have anything, I said.

Oh, but you will, you will.

Through the transparent plastic of one bag I could see a collection of hairbrushes and spoons.

Earlier that morning, Luna had told me that no one liked to share a cell with Aurora because of the odor from the fumigation canisters and because she hoarded everything. Luna said that her cellmates would leave the room as soon as they could and go to the patio or the large room where everyone gathered for classes and meals. This meant that Aurora had the cell to herself for the day. She slept most of the time.

Georgia called Aurora Sleeping Beauty, Luna said. She sleeps because she prefers dreams, not because she's tired. Aurora opens the spout on the fumigation canister and smells the poison, Luna continued. She takes the fumes deep into her body and this makes her sleepy. It's her sleeping potion.

As I sat on Aurora's bed, the smell was overpowering. The odor had penetrated her bed, belongings, clothes, and skin. No insect would ever come near her.

Do you have any aspirin? Aurora asked.

In that cluttered jail cell filled with poisonous fumes, I learned that Aurora met Paula at McClane's ranch.

The day Paula arrived it was McClane's daughter's fifteenth birthday party, Aurora said. I was in a tent with the other stolen women. Most of them had been taken when they tried to cross the border into the USA. All these men kept coming in and looking us over. I was already older. This was the third time I had been sold. Paula said she was from outside Acapulco. She was so beautiful.

I nodded. Yes, she was.

I thought of our angry piece of land that once held a

real community, but was ruined by the criminal world of drug traffickers and the immigration to the United States. Our angry piece of land was a broken constellation and each little home was ash.

Aurora struggled to breathe. She sat up on her elbows but stayed under the blankets. I perched on the edge of the bed, as there were so many bags and things around her. There was no room. Aurora's bed was a garbage dump.

A man who was the son of a huge drug lord in Tijuana took me, Aurora explained. Because of this, I did not live on McClane's ranch, but we would visit often and there were parties. Sometimes I would go to Matamoros or they would come to Tijuana. So, I didn't see Paula that often, but I saw her. I remember once I went to McClane's ranch for a birthday party and she had a tattoo that said *Cannibal's Baby* on her arm. I'd never seen that before. Of course, one of McClane's nicknames was Cannibal. They called him that because he was always making jokes about eating people, especially women.

Did he really eat people?

He'd say things like, You're so pretty, I want to eat your arm. I'll shake some salt on you and roll you up in a tortilla. Things like that. We all knew that when we gave ourselves to these men it was like washing dishes or taking out the garbage.

What do you mean?

It was like being a urinal.

Aurora coughed and reached for a plastic bottle filled with water and took a long drink. When she finished, she offered the bottle to me. I didn't want to, because she seemed so sick, but I took a sip. I knew I was drinking her spit.

Paula's tattoo was something new, Aurora continued. I

was surprised she had that done, but maybe she just had no choice.

Yes, she had that tattoo, I said. And the cigarette burns.

Those men loved tattoo parlors and they always went to one in Tijuana. McClane had Saint Death tattooed on his back and the Virgin of Guadalupe on his chest. I never saw Paula again and we never said goodbye.

She made it home. It was not expected.

The rumor was that she'd managed to run away. They said one night she just walked out of the ranch and walked and walked and never came back. We thought he might have killed her. You never knew. We hoped she had not tried to cross to the United States because she would have been stolen again for sure.

What happened to you? I asked as Aurora lay back on her bed. She had no pillow so she had to lie flat.

I took the rat poison out from under the kitchen sink and mixed it in with the coffee.

Aurora's eyes were so pale they made me think of the light blue color of dead jellyfish on the beach in Acapulco.

Where are you from? I asked.

Aurora was from Baja California. She grew up in the village of San Ignacio. Her father worked as a tour guide taking tourists out in his boat to see the California gray whales.

Look at this, Aurora said.

She pulled out a piece of cardboard from under her pile of plastic bags. It was a collage of a beach with a whale on the surface of the water and several starfish and shells cut out from magazines and glued to the brown sheet.

I cut the starfish from black paper, she said. No magazine in this jail had a photograph of a starfish!

I like it, I said. It's pretty. It reminds me of beaches on the outside of Acapulco. I've never seen a whale though.

You have to understand, the first time I was stolen I was only twelve, Aurora continued. I was only a small fish, the kind you always throw back into the ocean because it is too small to eat. They should not have done that! I was the only girl in the village with light eyes.

Her eyes were like the glass in a glass-bottom boat.

No one could believe it at the ranch. Who would ever have thought that Aurora, the sweetest and most obedient of all, could have done it, but I did.

I could see into Aurora's eyes and down into her body of light brown sand and shells.

I killed five men. Isn't that so special! They were gathered at the ranch for a meeting. It took them two days to die in a hospital in Tijuana. The police came and arrested me when the doctors proved that the men had been poisoned. The police tested the coffee cups and they tested positive for poison. And I'd even washed them over and over with Ajax! Everyone knew I made the coffee for the rats' meetings. Everyone knew there was a bottle of rat poison in the rats' kitchen under the sink. Rats need to be poisoned, right?

Aurora rummaged through one of her plastic supermarket bags. She unknotted a bag filled with buttons and a stack of nail files that were held together with a rubber band. From here she also pulled out a small pile of old newspaper clippings.

Here. Read this, if you don't believe me. It was even in the newspapers!

I read the newspaper article and then handed the clipping back to her and she placed it back into the pile.

She was proud of killing those men. It was her act of justice.

I boiled the water. I added the coffee. I let it sit.

Yes.

I placed the cups on a tray with a bowl of sugar. I could hear the men talking in the dining room. I stirred the coffee grounds in the pot.

Yes.

Aurora paused and tried to take a breath. She only seemed able to breathe out. She tried to breathe in not only with her lungs but also with her whole body, in heaves, but failed.

How did you do it?

It just took one minute. It was easy. I took out the bottle of rat poison from under the sink. I poured it into the coffee. It was so easy. It was like adding sugar or Coffee-mate.

I reached over and took her arm. The surface of her skin felt coarse as if it were still covered in beach sand. I looked into the sea landscape of her eyes and saw the whales and dolphins.

Please tell me more about Paula and McClane, I said.

Aurora told me that McClane not only had ranches all over the north, he also had businesses and properties in the state of Guerrero.

Near you, Aurora said. I never saw this, but other women told me that he had a mansion outside of Acapulco where one Christmas he built the North Pole and even brought in real reindeer on an airplane.

Yes, I answered, I've heard about that.

Did you know that McClane loved his horse so much that he buried it in a coffin in a cemetery as if it were a person?

No, I did not know that.

They say he wants to be buried in his car.

The cemeteries are full of men buried in their cars. I have heard about this.

I watched Aurora take another sip from the water bottle. How did Paula make it back? Aurora asked. Did you see her?

Aurora rested her head back down on the mattress.

Did she tell you about McClane's ranch? Aurora asked.

Paula's mother fed her from a bottle, a baby bottle, and even fed her baby food, Gerber, from a jar, I said.

Aurora listened and yawned. Her eyes closed and opened a few times. Then she turned on her side and fell asleep.

I looked at her. With her face quiet, in repose, without struggling to breathe, I could see she had been beautiful. She had been worth stealing. Today she was like a malnourished dog lost on the highway.

I curled up at the bottom of her bed among the plastic bags and fumigation canisters and fell asleep too.

For the first time in jail I had a dream. I knew the poisonous fumes had given me the dream. It was about Julio. We were lying on the grass, side by side, in the garden of the marble house in Acapulco. We lay on our sides looking at each other. I could see inside of his body. Under his flesh I saw the stars and the moon and I knew he was born from space.

The sound of Aurora coughing in her sleep awoke me. The light in the room was dim and I realized I'd been dozing there for several hours. It was as if being with someone who knew Paula, who knew something about my life, had given me the comfort to be able to sleep. Aurora had carried me home.

As I opened my eyes, I saw the shape of a person in the bed across from Aurora. It was Violeta.

I sat up.

She was naked and her hair was wrapped in a towel. I

could see a few drops of water trickle out from under the towel and behind her ear. On the floor there was a trail of water that led from the tiny shower stall to her bed.

On her bed, against the wall, she had many stuffed animals. In the pile I could make out a panda, a giraffe, and at least four teddy bears. It was a zoo.

Her body was covered in tattoos. Down the side of her upper arm that faced toward me I could see the word *Tom.* Around the wrist of that same arm she had tattooed bracelets that looked like barbed wire.

She was sitting cross-legged with another towel opened on the bed in front of her. On the towel she had a few ink jars. I could see red and green in the jars. She also had several syringes and long needles spread out on the cloth.

Violeta looked at me.

Good morning, she said.

Is it morning still?

Hey, don't you want a tattoo? Everyone in here has a tattoo. I've got the works here. I can carve you up.

When Violeta spoke, Aurora stirred and awoke.

No. Not yet, but thanks. If I walk out of here with a tattoo my mother will kill me!

Violeta, let her be, Aurora said.

Did anyone tell you, Princess, that on the outside people cry over you for exactly three days and then they forget you exist? Violeta said.

She reached over and pinched the skin of my upper arm. She took my skin between her fingers and turned it as if it were a key in a lock.

Stop! That hurts!

Why? she asked and let go of my arm. Why do good people always think they're right? Huh?

What did I say?

In here we are not people who turn the other cheek, she said.

Luna appeared at the doorstep. She was holding a thick beige-colored sweater in her hand. She held it out to me.

I got this for you. It's yours. One of us got out today and said I could have it. Here, put it on. It will keep you warm, Luna said.

I didn't even give it a thought. The jail was so cold I could feel my body turning into wet cement. I sat up, took the sweater, and pulled it over my head. It smelled like the body of another woman. It was like the smell of rice boiling on the stove.

Let me sleep, Aurora said. Please.

Violeta looked at Luna and then back to me. Here we sleep two in each bunk bed, head to foot, because it is better to sleep with someone's foot in one's mouth than their stinky face and bad jail breath.

Yes, Luna said. We know.

You two get to have your own bunks. That's not fair!

Stop it, Aurora said. Since when did you go looking around for the world to be fair?

Let's go. Come on, Luna said.

A tattoo will make you feel good, Violeta called out to me as we walked away. Think about it. I'm not expensive.

As I walked back to my cell with Luna at my side I thought this day was almost finished. My whole being was leaning toward Sunday, Visitors' Day. Only one more day and I would see my mother. I imagined that by now she was in a cheap hotel somewhere near the jail. I could feel it.

That Violeta! She's such a glutton, Luna said. When she eats chicken she feels love. When she eats a steak she feels happiness. I've seen her eat a whole cake.

Why did she kill all those men? I asked.

It was just part of her gluttony, Luna says. I figured it out. Killing was like eating.

As we walk, I tell Luna about my dream. I tell her that the universe was inside of Julio.

You need to thank God for resolving your destiny in the dream and thank Him for His warning, Luna said. A long time ago I promised God that I would heed every single one of His messages.

What do you think it means? I asked.

It's so obvious.

Well?

It means that you want to see the hands of the clock go backward. Back in time everyone is the same.

I don't think so. That is not what it means.

What does it mean then?

I think I know. When I know I will tell you.

When I climbed up to my bed that night, there was a photograph of Princess Diana in a black ball gown and a tiara on her head that had been torn out of a magazine and stuck to my wall with Scotch tape. The real loveliness of the dead princess beside my body in jail dressed in worn beige sweatpants made me feel ugly and dirty. I tore the photo off the wall and rolled it into a ball in my hand. The black ink of her ball gown stained my fingers.

Twenty-Four

The next morning Luna and I went out to the outdoor patio and sat in a streak of sunshine. Almost everyone on the patio was looking for a ray of sunlight to warm their bodies. The long shadow cast by the men's jail made most of the open yard sunless.

By eleven the patio was filled with women standing in groups talking while by the southern wall a football game had begun. I could see Georgia's yellow hair running after the ball and Violeta on the sidelines watching the game. Luna bought a cup of coffee for both of us from a woman who sold coffee and sweet bread out of a basket.

Luna wanted to watch the football game and I did not. So I strolled over to a bench and sat down while she went to the other side of the patio to stand with Violeta.

I sipped on the lukewarm coffee and, after a few moments, I watched Aurora walk out of the prison building onto the patio. She squinted and flinched in the outdoor light as if it hurt her eyes.

I waved for her to come and sit with me. She moved slowly, on tiptoe, as if she were walking in slow motion or miming what it was to walk. The fumigation canister was on her back and she wore it as if it were a turtle shell.

She sat next to me and was barefoot. It was her feet hurting against the icy cement that had made her walk like that. She sat beside me and I gave her what was left of my coffee.

Here, you can finish it, I said.

Her pale, dry hand wrapped around the Styrofoam cup and exposed the pattern of cigarette burns on the inside of her arm. In the patio light the round scars looked like mother-of-pearl moons.

Where are your shoes?

Someone is always stealing my stuff. This morning they were gone.

Her feet looked stiff and blue. I was still wearing my plastic flip-flops. If I had shoes would I give them to her? I knew I probably wouldn't. In only a few days the jail had modified me. I thought about what Violeta had said earlier, how people outside forgot you in only three days.

I took the canister off Aurora's back and made her sit facing me on the bench. I placed her feet on my lap and covered them with my sweater.

Now we both need shoes, I said.

The truth was that, now when I looked at Aurora, after everything she'd told me about Paula, it was as if she were a road out of jail, through the streets of Mexico City, to the black highway and back to my home.

Aurora drained the last of the coffee, placed the empty cup on the floor, and then reached for my hand and held it. Even though Aurora was older than me, she was like a child. Her hand was small like a seven-year-old's. I held on to it as if I were going to help her cross a street.

Aurora continued to speak as if our conversation from

the day before had not been interrupted by a sudden exhausted sleep. The poison sleep.

We could not believe that Paula would run away, Aurora said. He would find her. She knew that. He would find her eventually. She knew that.

I don't think he's found her, I answered. Paula and her mother disappeared. They left. They're hiding somewhere. No one knows where.

Aurora took her hand out of my hand and hugged her stomach as if it hurt.

You don't understand, she said.

What?

My stomach hurts. My head hurts.

Is there a doctor here?

Only on Mondays. I don't want to see him. He might not let me fumigate and then how will I make money?

It's making you sick.

It makes me dream and sleep. But you don't understand, she said again. Ladydi, you don't understand.

What?

Aurora rocked back and forth holding her stomach. Her eyes rolled back and I could see the whites of her eyes.

Listen, she whispered.

Listen, she whispered again. When you killed McClane why did you kill Paula's little girl too? Why?

I'm sorry. I don't understand. What?

When you killed McClane, when you killed Juan Rey Ramos, you know. What were you thinking? When you killed McClane why did you kill Paula's little girl too? Why?

The words she spoke stood still in the air as if they were cooked with the poison she breathed in and out of her lungs. I felt as if I could reach out and catch the words suspended in the air and break them up in my hands like dry leaves. I could taste poison in my mouth.

When you killed McClane why did you kill Paula's little girl too? Why?

I had seen the dresses drying on the maguey cactus. I had imagined the narrow, twig arms of a little girl coming out of the sleeves. They were almost dry and so they lifted and blew in the heat. On the ground beside the cactus there was a toy bucket and a toy broom.

When you killed McClane why did you kill Paula's little girl too? Why?

Blood could smell like roses.

When you killed McClane why did you kill Paula's little girl too? Why?

I closed my eyes and prayed to the radio. I prayed to the song on the radio, the song I had heard again and again in Acapulco. I heard it when I cleaned the house. I heard it on the beach. I heard it in the glass-bottom boat. I heard it. I heard it. I heard the narco ballad for Juan Rey Ramos:

Even dead he's the most powerful man alive,
Even dead he's the most powerful man alive.
The pistol that killed him also killed his girl,
And you'll see their ghosts alive, pale as pearl.
Together, hand-in-hand, on the highway,
Together, hand-in-hand, on the highway.
For God save your prayers, don't speak a word,
We sing for the man and the child butchered.

Twenty-Five

On Sunday morning most of the prisoners woke up early to get ready for Visitors' Day. The women painted their fingernails, combed their hair into buns and braids or straightened it out with large curlers that they'd worn on their heads all night. Even prisoners who never had visitors would get fixed up just in case.

What everyone did know was that the queue of visitors waiting to get in outside the women's jail was short. The queue for visitors to the men's jail was long and went way down the road and covered a distance of at least ten blocks. It could take hours for visitors to finally get in and see the men.

It was Luna who had told me this.

There is nothing else one needs to know about anything, she said. No one visits the women. Everyone visits the men. What more do we need to know about the world?

The jail rules at the women's prison were that the visitors were brought in to the patio first and, half an hour later, the prisoners were allowed out.

At eleven we queued up in the corridor that led out to the yard. I was pressed between Luna and Georgia in single file. Georgia had a huge wad of bubble gum in her mouth and I could hear it snap as she moved it around.

Do you have any more of that? I asked.

I had not brushed my teeth since I'd arrived.

Georgia pulled out a piece of pink gum from a pocket in her jeans and gave it to me.

Thank you.

Hold on to your prayers, she said, every religion known to man comes here on Sunday and wants to steal them.

Outside the patio was completely transformed. It was like a fairground. Everyone was dressed in reds and yellows. Visitors were not allowed to wear blue or beige so that they would not accidently get mistaken for a prisoner.

The space was filled with people carrying baskets of food and presents wrapped in bright-colored paper. To one side there were four nuns dressed in white habits waiting on a bench. There were many children running around. I expected to see a balloon man or a cotton-candy vendor appear at any moment.

Scanning over the drab prisoner colors and brightly colored visitors, I looked for my mother.

I didn't see her.

She did not come.

And then I saw my father walking toward me.

I walked toward him through jungle leaves.

Iguanas scurried away as I moved under papaya trees and broke spiderwebs that grew across my path.

I could smell the orange blossoms in the trees around me.

It was not my father.

Maria opened her arms and, as they opened, I could see the ugly round scar on her upper arm and the huge chunk of missing flesh left from my mother's gunshot. I could also see the faint scar on her upper lip left from the operation on her harelip.

I walked into her embrace. She kissed my cheek.

For the first time in my life I thought, Thank you, Daddy. Thank you, Daddy. Thank you for fucking around and giving me Maria.

I took Maria's hand and walked her to one side of the patio, far from everyone. All the benches were taken and so we sat down on the cement ground with our backs resting against the wall that divided the area from the men's prison.

I could see Luna sitting with the nuns. Georgia and Violeta were talking to a woman in a gray business suit. I didn't see Aurora anywhere.

At least you're safe here, Maria said.

Maria told me that her mother was dead. Maria had hid in the hole and listened to a group of men fire machine guns at her house and into the body of her mother.

I was saved by the hole. Imagine, Maria said. The hole saved someone.

It saved me once too.

The trees and grass were covered in her blood, Maria continued. I knew if I looked up, the sky would be covered in her blood. I know the moon is covered in her blood. It always will be.

I caressed Maria's hair in long strokes from the top of her head down to her neck. Maria shivered.

I didn't dare come out of the hole for days, she said. I would look up at the sky from the hole and see the vultures.

Yes.

I could hear the ants moving.

Yes.

After four days, I was so thirsty, I couldn't cry.

Yes, I know.

I was so alone.

Yes.

I heard one man say, be grateful we are killing you. It could be worse.

Yes.

My mother knew I was in the hole. Kill me, she said.

Yes, you can keep on telling me. Tell me more, I said.

I was in that hole for days. When I looked up, the sky was covered in blood.

And then what did you do?

I ran to your mother's house. Where else could I go? Where else could I go? She took care of me and let me sleep in your bed.

I placed my arm around Maria.

The ground here is so cold, she said.

Yes, in this place even the sun is cold.

As we sat on the cement in the meager sunlight, glass began to fall out of the sky. Glass dust fell from the stars.

Everyone in the yard looked up at the clouds.

There was silence.

The shards fell and children held out their hands and caught the dust. The crystal glittered. The ground and all surfaces were covered in glass snow.

The Popocatepetl volcano had dropped its cloud of ash on our prison.

Twenty-Six

One of the senior prison guards came out in the yard and announced to the visitors that they had to leave and told the prisoners they had to get inside. The volcanic ash was filled with microscopic shards that could cut up your lungs and eyes.

Maria and I stood up. Our dark hair had turned a gray white from the ash.

Did you know Paula had had a baby? It was McClane's.

No.

Mike killed Paula's child. I was with him that day. And he killed McClane.

Maria covered her mouth with her hand. This was a gesture she'd always made to hide her harelip. Even after the operation she continued to hide her broken face.

They'll find us, she said behind the gate of her fingers.

Her body began to tremble.

I sat in Mike's car, I said. I didn't know. I wasn't in there.

Did you see the girl?

I saw her dresses. Where's my mother?

She's here. She's done the paperwork. You're not eighteen. You can't be here.

I'll go to the juvenile jail for a year and then I'll be back here. I've learned all about that. It's how it works, Maria.

You're out tomorrow. She didn't want to see her baby in jail like a jungle bird, or like a wild parrot, in a cage. That's what she said. Those words.

Where is she?

At the hotel. She told me to tell you that love is not a feeling. It's a sacrifice.

Yes.

I'll see you tomorrow.

Yes.

Stay in the shadows. Don't get into trouble. Walk in the shadows.

Goodbye.

Here's a bar of soap.

Can you give me something?

What?

Give me your earrings.

Maria was wearing a pair of plastic pearl studs. She did not ask what for, which I loved. She had always been like that. She never asked why. Maria assumed you knew what you were talking about.

Maria took off her earrings and dropped them in my hand.

See you tomorrow, she said.

Maria stood and I watched her as she walked through the crowd of robbers and killers to the exit.

She walked in the glass snow.

That night I gave Luna the earrings.

Thank you, Luna said. Do not try and rhyme, you know, understand, anything that happened to you here.

Twenty-Seven

The Gods were angrier than we thought, my mother said.

These were the first words she spoke to me. She didn't expect an answer.

Outside the jail I walked through a landscape where there were no trees or flowers. It was a terrain of discarded clothes as if the land had become cloth. I walked through the beige and blue fabric prisoners had stripped off their bodies and left behind in the street.

Volcanic ash still covered most surfaces and our steps left footprints in the glass powder.

My mother handed me a red sweater. I threw the worn sweatshirt Luna had given me on the ground where it became part of the blue-and-beige patchwork.

Outside the jail's parking lot my mother had a taxi waiting for us. Maria was sitting inside. We got in the back seat beside her. I sat between them. Maria placed her arm around me.

To the South Station bus terminal, my mother said to the taxi driver.

Take off those flip-flops, my mother said.

She took a pair of tennis shoes out of her bag and reached down and pulled the sandals off my feet as if I were a little girl. Then she threw the flip-flops out the window as if they were candy wrappers.

Where are we going, Mama?

I'm going to wash all the dishes in the United States, my mother said.

We're not going to wait around, Maria said. You have a meeting with the Social Services later today and they will probably place you in a juvenile delinquency center.

As soon as you turn eighteen, they place you right back in that jailbird birdhouse, my mother said.

I thought of Luna's words about immigrants going to the United States. I could see my mother, Maria, and me swimming across the river.

Shit, think of *The Sound of Music*! my mother said. It will be like that.

Yes, Maria said.

We're going to the USA and I am going to wash dishes. I will wash all the dishes, all that steak blood and cake icing. You're going to be a nanny to a family. You and Maria can be nannies. And we will never tell anyone where we came from.

Yes, Maria said.

Do you know why?

Why? I asked.

We're not telling where we came from. It's simple, my mother said. It's simple because no one will ever ask.

Mama, I said, I have something for you. I stole something for you.

I opened my hand and took off the diamond ring and gave it to her. She looked at it without saying a word. She placed it on her finger.

You have made me love my hand, she said.

It's beautiful, Maria said.

Someone cast a net across this country and we fell in it, my mother said.

As we drove through the city's streets, through the traffic and diesel fumes of the large trucks, I watched my mother stare at the ring and pet the large diamond with her finger.

Along the avenue the street sweepers, with their mouths covered by handkerchiefs, were cleaning up the ash. They brushed it into large black plastic garbage bags. These bags were piled up like boulders at every corner.

There's something I need to tell you, I said. There are five people in this taxi.

I pointed to my belly.

There's a baby in here, I said.

My mother didn't blink or breathe or move and then she kissed my cheek. Maria kissed my other cheek.

They kissed me, but they did not kiss me.

They were already kissing my child.

My mother said, Just pray it's a boy.

Acknowledgments

Prayers for the Stolen was written thanks to a National Endowment for the Arts (NEA) Fellowship in Fiction and the support of Mexico's Sistema Nacional de Creadores de Arte (FONCA).

HOGARTH
LONDON · NEW YORK

In 1917 Virginia and Leonard Woolf started The Hogarth Press from their Richmond home, Hogarth House, armed only with a hand-press and a determination to publish the newest, most inspiring writing. They went on to publish some of the twentieth century's most significant writers, joining forces with Chatto & Windus in 1946.

Inspired by their example, Hogarth is a new home for a new generation of literary talent; an adventurous fiction imprint with an accent on the pleasures of storytelling and a keen awareness of the world. Hogarth is a partnership between Chatto & Windus in the UK and Crown in the US, and our novels are published from London and New York.

22:00
28
OSTIRALA
da en
G. Romero
sobre el líquido imponible de
1
CD + DVD
(que contiene
¡PAPÁ NO
DIVORCIES
BARRILITO